J.B. WILLIAMS

The City of Clouds

First published by JB Writes Stuff 2023

Second Print, October 2024

First edition

ISBN: 979-8-9895133-1-4

Editing by Stephen Zimmer

This book was professionally typeset on Reedsy.
Find out more at reedsy.com

Contents

Robin Alia Brook

Planet: ANDROMEDA
  System: FURIES
  Sector: PROSPECT
  Date: 27-JAN-2429

Robin Alia Brook's first requested day off in three years has been shot in the face. It is not because she was at work. She did get a message asking if she can come into work to cover a shift and get a different day off in exchange, but she politely declined. The reason being that she at a restaurant called Poseidon, and it's located five hundred feet below the surface of the Cepheus Sea in Lower Cepheus City. She had plans to dine there with her date, but so far, he is three hours late. In the meantime, she's surviving on a steady diet of free lemon water and cheesy seaweed and black powder biscuits.

Robin spends her time watching the posh waiters escort wealthy customers to their tables, each adorned with a small lamp to illuminate the dim restaurant. Across from her, a bald man dressed in mismatched stripes and spots eats alone while scribbling in his notebook.

Robin struggles to hold back her tears and takes a sip of water, feeling like an abandoned puppy as she watches people come and go. Through the window, she sees a school of fish swim by and hears light chatter and laughter drifting through the filtered air.

A door opens. Robin perks, and a new couple walks in and talks to a waiter, who grabs a pair of menus and escorts them to their destination.

Robin puts her water down and lays her head on the table, staring at a model of a sail ship traversing the high seas. While the details are phenomenal, Robin can't help but wonder why she went through so much trouble just to be stood up. She could have gotten holiday pay instead of being miserable for free. She even came as her very best.

Her skin was scrubbed clean with charcoal soap and her long, dark hair washed with the finest products. She made sure to clean her chocolate-colored eyes with drops and enhance her lashes before donning high-end finger-less gloves (protected by plastic gloves), a black jacket with an ivory buttoned-cuff, a white dress shirt, a black and white tie, and matching pants and shoes, all tailored to emphasize her slender, feminine figure. But all of this effort was for nothing as she was ultimately stood up.

The door opens again, spilling warm light into the room, and Robin's head lifts, just for it to slam on the table again when more strangers walk in. Then, the waiter that has been keeping her company approaches the table with a pitcher of water and small plate of biscuits.

"Ma'am, you've been here for three hours... I don't think your date is showing up. You probably got stood up and should go home," says the waiter.

"That's rude customer service," says Robin, without taking her head off the table. She pushes the empty cup to the waiter. "Fill it, please."

"You do know we might have to charge you a little bit for all the free water and biscuits you consumed, right?"

"I don't care."

"Alright, suit yourself."

The waiter sets the plate down and fills Robin's cup. After he leaves, Robin sluggishly pulls out her phone and turns on a messaging app. There is her face, smiling brightly next to a rising sun and the expansive sea. Below her is a sandy haired man with a big bear and sunglasses, and a dog. She begins typing with shaky fingers, and her wet eyes drift between her phone and the door.

Robin: *So... about meeting me at Poseidon...*

Robin sends the message, and immediately after...

Cliff: *Yeah?*

Robin frowns and types faster.

Robin: *I'm here and waiting for you.*

Cliff: *Wait... Right now?*

Robin: *Yes.*

Cliff: *"Right now" right now?*

Robin: *YES!*

Five minutes later.

Cliff: *No, you aren't.*

Robin growls, snaps a picture of herself while fish swim by her window, and sends her bloodshot eyes and twisted frown to Cliff.

Nothing happens.

Robin throws her phone down and drinks her water. Her hand grips the cup tight, her foot rapidly taps the floor, shaking her chair and table, and passing waiters give her worried looks.

Ten minutes later, she gets a response from Cliff.

Cliff: *Oh shit... Yeah, this is awkward. I thought you were fake.*

Robin is drinking again when she sees this, and she slams her cup down, growling, thus drawing all eyes to her, and her hands tremble as she types.

Robin: *FKAE!*

Robin: *FAKE!?*

Robin: *Hw do you thkin Im fake!*

Robin: *Why did you think I'm fake!*

Robin: *I was fake?*

Cliff: *I mean, I thought you were a chat-bot because dating apps are bot farms that siphon information and money, and I was just talking to you because I was bored. Even though I thought you were a bot.*

Robin: *OMG*

Cliff: *But now that I know you're real, we can schedule something. Diner and a movie? Walk on the beach? I'm on Oros right now, so I'm a little far from Andromeda, but I can request a job over there again. Me and my boss are cool with each other, so it won't be too hard to come over.*

Robin jumps up and waves at her waiter, face hot and wet from tears. "Waiter! Bill me!" yells Robin.

The waiter nods and hurries away for his task, and Robin resumes typing.

Robin: *It's dinner and a movie. And no. You're mean! I'm real! I've always been real, and you're mean and a jerk! BLOCKED!*

And keeping to her word, Robin blocks Cliff, grabs her purse, pays for her excessive free water and biscuits, and storms out of the restaurant. As she leaves, the patrons and waiters stare at her.

Robin hurries through a tunnel with bright lights and maps, heading to an elevator station. Her vision is blurry, her chest heavy, and her eyes burning. As she rapidly hits the button for the elevator, she sniffs and quivers. She slides inside when the door opens and quickly presses the close button. She thinks she sees someone running towards the elevator, but the doors close before they can reach them.

Not that she cares, anyway. She just wants to be alone.

The doors click and a bell dings as a sign lights up, instructing Robin to sit down and buckle up. So, she does exactly that, and her foot rapidly taps the floor as the elevator pod shifts and hums while the interior is bathed in red.

Robin wipes her eyes, smearing her makeup, and bangs her head on the elevator pod's wall. Next to her is a sign advertising a habitat where various orbs surrounding a large orb, all connected by rings and tubes, float above a gas giant with what Robin can only assume are a husband and wife, smiling brightly and pointing at it. Below it are some blocky words.

"The Future Is in the City of Clouds! Sign Up and Win a Vacation Lottery Today!"

On the other side is a wanted poster for information about a group called "Crow's Murder," and with it, a multitude of small profile shots surrounding a dark-skinned man with braided hair, light brown eyes, and black feathers tattooed on his cheeks. His name is Crow Magnolia, with a reward of eight hundred million fedos. Everyone else is named with significantly smaller rewards, but Robin isn't paying any attention to them.

The only reason she noticed Crow's Murder was because his picture was staring at her when she entered. But that said, she doesn't care about Crow Magnolia, his pirates, or about *The City of Clouds*, or anybody or anything. She just wants to go home.

Ding!

The noise makes Robin jump in her seat. The lights change to green, and the sign gives permission to unbuckle. Robin unbuckles, and the door slides open, revealing heavy rain pouring on a group of people waiting outside, under a nearby gazebo.

Robin exits, the pedestrians enter, and Robin walks down the sidewalk of Upper Cepheus City. Heavy rain soaks her body and pushes her hair in front of her eyes. Lightning flashes in the distance. Rain crashes down on the pavement of the urban jungle of twisting metal and glass monoliths, and Robin ascends a flight of stairs that are next to a monorail track. She grips the rail tight as she takes careful steps up. The railing has warning signs and messages of replacement glass panels coming soon.

When Robin reaches the top of the stairs, a man wearing a hoodie and a mask suddenly jumps out from behind one of the raised concrete beds and grabs Robin's purse, while aiming a gun at her face.

"GIVE ME YOUR PURSE!" yells the criminal.

Robin shrieks and recoils, tugging the criminal with her. They both slip on the stairs, and Robin manages to grab the handrail while the criminal tumbles down the stairs.

Robin cringes as she watches him fall, and he bounces off the stairway wall and crashes through a glass panel of the railing. He screams as he falls with the broken glass and lands on the monorail track below, snapping his neck and spine.

Robin crawls to the edge and peeks over, gasping from horror as the rail's electric currents surge through the criminal's body and ignite him, turning his body into a torch in seconds.

Then, a monorail runs over the charred body. Robin recoils and presses herself against the stair wall and covering her mouth as her wide, wet eyes stare ahead.

Sirens wail in the distance, and Robin's drop while she stares ahead, in a state of shock, unable to move, hardly able to breathe, and her heart beating fast enough to tear itself apart.

Red and blue lights approach, and Robin leans forward and grips her head tight with tears dripping into the flood cascading down the stairs.

"Oh dear... I'm in so much trouble," says Robin.

One Year Later

Planet: ANDROMEDA
  System: FURIES
  Sector: PROSPECT
  Date: 27-JAN-2430

Robin lays flat on her bed, back sinking into the mattress, hands folded on her stomach, and her wide dead eyes staring at the ceiling. She is still dressed fabulously and is cleaned to optimal standards, but after a long day of work, she has decided it is best to pretend that she was dead.

On her nightstand is her phone, with her Arx Corporation employee badge next to it. Her smiling face in the badge photo is a stark contrast to the gloomy, disheveled look Robin currently has. Her phone is blinking with a green rotary phone icon shaking, but it is silent, and Robin's eyes don't register the green light flashing on the wall.

The phone icon disappears after ten seconds, and a wall of notifications takes up her screen. Mostly from dating apps, but there are other notifications from her emails, voice mails, text messages, news updates about pirate attacks, and the weather.

The weather app is kind enough to let her know that Cepheus City is having heavy rain, even though Robin already knew that because of the storm beating against her window. Just like last year, when the criminal fell on the tracks, snapped his bones, ignited, and got pulverized by the monorail train.

She can still see his smoldering flesh and hear his bones being crushed and can smell the burnt blood and muscle. The police and people at work tried to comfort her and tell her that what happened was not her fault, but they are wrong. If she had just let the guy take her purse, then he would still be alive, and she wouldn't have nightmares. No death, no nightmares, and no mess for the city to take care of.

A sudden knocking on the door breaks Robin's thoughts, but she remains motionless. The knocking returns, and without looking, Robin grabs her phone and stiffly check the camera to see who is outside.

It is her adopted parents. One is an Asian woman with bleached-blonde hair and pale skin, and the other is a muscular white man with brownish-gray hair cut down to the fuzz, and his skin is tanned from the long hours outside. She remotely unlocks the door to let them in.

The door clicks, light from the hallway seeps into the studio apartment, and her adopted parents walk in. Her father is Brent Brook, a longtime loyal officer of the Cepheus City Police Department. Her mother is Emerald Brook, an accountant for Arx Corporation.

"Robin are you okay? Why is it so dark in here?" asks Emerald.

"I just got back from work and didn't feel like living," says Robin, still staring at the ceiling.

Brent turns on the lights, burning Robin's eyes. She grabs one of her pillows and puts it over her face to shield herself from the wrath of the nine-hundred-lumen light bulbs.

"Well, Robin, you might want to see the mail that came to our apartment instead of yours," says Brent.

Robin keeps the pillow over her face, but Brent easily yanks it off and drops an envelope on her face. She reluctantly sits up and studies the paper, seeing a note from the one and only Cliff Birdie. She begrudgingly opens it and finds a ticket and a typed note.

Dear Robin,

Sorry for how things ended. I know it has been a year, but I never really forgave myself for what happened. So, enclosed is a winning vacation lottery ticket for The City of Clouds. Originally, I was going to go, but I couldn't help but think about how badly things ended, so I'm giving this to you instead. All the transfer stuff has been taken care of. Enjoy your time.

–Cliff Birdie

Robin drops the letter and ticket on her lap and stares off into space. Her adopted parents stare at her quietly, and the void in her eyes remains, while the rain beats heavily against the windows.

"Is everything okay?" asks Emerald.

"I just got a winning vacation lottery ticket to *The City of Clouds*," says Robin blankly.

"I didn't know you signed up for the vacation lottery. That's great that you won!" says Emerald.

"But I didn't sign up for a ticket. My ex did. He just gave it to me. But I don't want to go on vacation anyway. I just want to stay in here and stare at my ceiling," says Robin.

"Why? It's **The City of Clouds!** A jewel of the Prospect Sector **and** the Furies System!" says Emerald.

"I just don't want to go," says Robin.

"When you said 'ex,' do you mean that guy that stood you up at the restaurant?" asks Brent.

Robin nods.

"Ah, well, he's forgiven now in my book," says Brent. "He's still a dick, but now he's a small one instead of a big one."

Robin holds the ticket out to her parents.

"You take it," says Robin.

Emerald gently pushes the ticket back to Robin.

"We don't need it or want it," says Emerald.

"I don't want it or need it either," says Robin.

"Yeah, you do."

"No, I don't!"

"The ticket's for one person anyway. And buying another one is too expensive."

"Fine, then I'll give it to someone at work."

"And who do you know at work well enough to give a winning vacation lottery ticket to?"

Robin thinks... And thinks... And thinks some more. Her parents stare at her patiently while she searches for names, but none come up. She eventually looks down with a dejected sigh, and Emerald points at her with a stern expression.

"Exactly. You're a recluse. You don't know anybody, and despite you dressing fashionably, you never attempt to make any friends. You're like a pretty bird that refuses to sing. How do birds get other birds? They sing and socialize!" says Emerald.

"But Cliff..." says Robin meekly.

Emerald rubs her chin. "True... But that was a fluke! People will hurt other people just because they can."

"Okay, that's enough of that. I think I know the real reason why Robin is reluctant to go on vacation," says Brent.

"You do?" asks Emerald.

"Of course!" Brent grabs Robin's shoulders and looks deep into her chocolate-brown eyes. "Robin, if you're worried about accidentally killing someone, then you need to snap out of it. That guy that you killed was a scumbag and you did the community a favor when you broke his spine on the tracks to get chewed up by the train. Besides, what're the chances of you accidentally killing someone again?"

Robin's eyes bulge and water, and Emerald slaps Brent's arm.

"Stop it! You suck at this!" says Emerald. Then she smiles warmly at Robin and speaks in a softer tone. "Robin, honey, you've been underneath a dark cloud for too long. You need to go on vacation, loosen up. Maybe you'll meet someone over there to be your special bird."

"But I have dating apps," says Robin.

As soon as she says that, her phone beeps and a wall of notifications for five dating apps takes up the screen, with one being from a person named DynamicDomino4D4, for an app called *Dating Universe*. Robin peeks at her phone, and quickly swipes them away when she sees their location is Venus; and she quickly swipes away the other notifications and clicks her screen to darken. After that, she turns back to her parents, who are less than amused by the interruption.

"Robin, dating apps are fake and gay," says Brent.

"We met on a dating app," says Emerald, staring at Brent out of the corner of her eye.

Brent scoffs. "Yeah, accidentally, and that was after I went through eight hundred and ninety-two bots and spent triple that in fedos. We just got lucky." Then he grabs Robin's arms and peers into her eyes again. "But Robin, sweetie, take the vacation. Don't worry about meeting anybody, don't worry about the dating apps, don't worry about that guy you accidentally killed, just live your life as if you're going to die tomorrow."

Robin sighs heavily and looks down, and Emerald hits him over the head with a pillow.

"Enough! You're terrible at this!" says Emerald.

"No, he's right. I'll go," says Robin reluctantly. "I can't be cooped up in here forever."

"That's the spirit!" says Brent.

"It better be because you want to enjoy life instead of fear death," says Emerald.

"Why not both?" asks Robin.

"Good enough," says Brent.

Emerald grabs the ticket from Robin and inspects it. "Let's see... The vacation is for three weeks, two weeks for travel time there and back again, and one week for actual stay, all expenses paid with fifty percent off food and beverages. And you must be at the spaceport on March fourteenth. Ah, so you have plenty of time to get situated!"

Brent takes the ticket and reads it over. When he is done, he smiles at Emerald while returning the ticket to Robin.

"That's a generous lottery. Maybe we should sign up for it next year?" says Brent.

"I agree," says Emerald. Then she looks at Robin and says, "As for you, what are you going to do?"

"I'm going to go on vacation," says Robin reluctantly.

"And...?"

Robin is silent, and Emerald frowns while Brent cranks his hand to motion Robin to speak.

"*And?*" repeats Emerald.

"Enjoy myself," grumbles Robin.

Emerald claps her hands. "That's right. Now, do you want to grab lunch?"

"And a movie?" adds Brent. "The Cinema Citadel is showing a screen adaptation of the mythical story, Die Hard!"

"Eh... Sure," says Robin.

"Good!" says Brent.

Brent wraps his arms around Emerald's shoulder while Robin grabs her phone, a plastic poncho, and an umbrella. When she is standing by her adopted parents, the three head to the hallway.

"But we're ordering cheap at Klumsy K's and we're only having drinks at the theater," instructs Brent.

"I can pay for myself," says Robin.

"But you won't. So don't worry about it."

"Can I at least tip?"

"Sure, as long as it does not exceed five percent."

And with that said, they ventured out into the storm to enjoy their time together.

Sparrow's Flock

Planet: ANDROMEDA
System: FURIES
Sector: PROSPECT
Date: 14-MAR-2430

First Landing Island, Interstellar Launch Port

The weather is pleasant, the sun is out and partially covered by white clouds, and a sleek white vehicle finds a nearby empty lot in a cramped parking lot near the launch port. the Robin comes out of the back and her adopted parents come out of the front. Brent pulls out a large case on wheels from the trunk and hands it off to Robin, then they go to the terminal where the buses wait.

The buses are bulbous with destinations scrolling across their digital screens, and each is guarded by a pair of guards wearing full masks and armored vests with wrist-top computers and rectangular communication devices on their shoulders. By each bus is a kiosk where people are submitting their tickets.

When Robin's group reaches the kiosk, Robin submits her vacation lottery ticket through a slot, and there is a whir and click, and the ticket is returned with four QR codes in the corner above her name.

They go to the guards, where Robin gives one her ticket. He scans it with a handheld device, and then stamps another QR code on it. After that, he looks at Brent and Emerald.

"Tickets?" asks the guard.

"Sorry, no. We're just dropping her off," says Emerald.

"Understood. But this is as far as you two go."

Emerald nods and hugs Robin.

"Have fun up there," says Emerald.

"I'll try," says Robin.

Emerald pulls away and Brent hugs Robin immediately after.

"What she said," says Brent.

Robin giggles. "I'll try."

Brent and Emerald back away, and Robin goes on the bus. The interior is spacious, so there is plenty of space for people and luggage. Robin takes a seat by the window so she can see her parents. They're still there, and a few more people are having their tickets scanned. The process takes a few minutes, but once the bus is full, the doors close and the door locks.

"Attention everyone, please remain seated while the bus is in motion. Failure to do so will result in a fine of seven hundred and fifty fedos and seven days in a probation cell. Thank you," says the bus driver over the intercom.

Robin and many other passengers buckle up. The bus moves forward with a hiss and hum, and Robin waves at her parents until she can no longer see them. Then, she sits stiffly in her seat and tightly grips her case's handle while trying to regulate her breathing with moderate success.

A few minutes later, her bus, and many others, come to a gradual stop in front of a large, pyramid-shaped structure with large glass planes reflecting the sunlight and fluffy clouds overhead.

"Destination reached. Enjoy your flights," says the bus driver over the intercom as the doors open.

The passengers file out in an orderly manner, and Robin goes to the side to take a breather by a rotating pillar advertising multiple spaceflight companies. Her heart is heavy and beating quickly, and her breathing is unsteady. People pass by her without stopping, she takes another deep breath, and forces herself to go forward.

Robin zigzags through the crowd as they scurry to their destinations, passing humans of various origins, an alien every now and then, and more advertisements, including one for pilots for the Strike Craft Force. This one is next to a table where men in uniform make attempts to entice passing young men with pitches of grandeur and patriotism.

After a few minutes of maneuvering through the crowd, Robin enters an area with a large tube neighbored by a smaller tube, both being guarded by soldiers and a hovering, orb-shaped machine. The soldier waves them forward while the conveyor belt for the other tube turns on.

"Fifteen in," orders the soldier.

Robin and fourteen others put their luggage on a conveyor belt leading to the smaller tube and uniformly enter the large one in uniform fashion. The tube closes, plunging everyone into darkness, and a blue grid appears and slides over the occupiers. A few seconds later, it slides over her again, this time from the back. Once the grid reaches its starting point, it dings, and the door opens. The group files out, grabs their luggage, and continues to their destination. As Robin travels, she pulls out her ticket and looks at the numbers.

"Terminal 3A-I-B. Row 18. Seat 4," says Robin to herself.

Robin looks up and sees a brightly lit sign saying **3A-I-B**, and she picks up her speed.

Then her body collides with someone. She stumbles back and drops her ticket, and the person she bumped into also stumbles.

"Oh dear, I'm sorry!" says Robin. She snatches her ticket off the floor and looks up with a sheepish smile. "That was my fault, I wasn't paying attention."

"That's alright. I've been through worse," says the man, a person with tanned skin, curly dark hair, and thin amount of facial hair to cover his blocky head. He is also wearing a simple suit, carrying a bland case, and has a badge hanging around his neck. He brushes himself off, but when he looks at Robin, he freezes, and his dark eyes widen as though he's seeing a ghost.

"That's a relief. Or not. I don't know," says Robin, oblivious to his expression.

The man blinks and replaces his odd look with a small smile.

"Do you talk to people often?" he asks.

"I talk to humans a lot," says Robin.

Robin's phone beeps, notifying her of another slew of dating apps and weather notifications. One of the notifications is from *Star Crossed*, and the username is Grandpanator1000, but he is way too old for Robin's taste, so she discards the notification. Robin clears off the rest of her notifications and sees a ticket on the floor. She snatches it, studies it, and looks at the stranger.

"By any chance, are you also 3A–I–B?" asks Robin.

The man holds out his hand. "Yes. That is my ticket."

Robin hands it to him, and she clears her throat nervously. "Well... Bye, I guess."

Robin is about to leave but stops when he calls her.

"Wait, ma'am," he says.

Robin turns to him, and he stuffs his ticket in his inner coat pocket and smiles anxiously.

"We've still got some time before our flight. Want to grab a bite and a drink at the deli while we wait?" he asks.

Robin stares at him for a few seconds, weighing the pros and cons of this, and then she looks at a nearby deli. After another few seconds of staring, she looks back at him and shrugs nervously.

"I guess so...?" says Robin.

"Oh good. I'm happy about that," he says with a heavy sigh of relief. "What?"

He waves Robin forward. "I mean, after you."

*****

A few minutes have passed, and Robin and the man are sitting at a booth, their backs to the crowd, cases by their feet, both nursing sodas while they wait for their meals.

"So... not to be awkward, but I completely spaced on asking your name," says Robin.

"My name is Ibis. Ibis Ajam," says the man.

"My name is Robin Brook."

Ibis extends his hand. "Nice to meet you, Robin."

Robin shakes Ibis's hand.

"Are you from around here?" asks Ibis.

"Born and raised on Andromeda. And you're from...?" says Robin.

"I'm from Alkhatib, Greater Arabia."

A waitress slides two sandwiches to them. Robin's is a small, simple sandwich, but Ibis's is a meat sandwich with bacon and lots of cheese, and whole wheat bread. Robin then slips on plastic gloves, on top of her expensive gloves, which brings Ibis to raise a brow.

"Alkhatib? That's been under Drevi control for thirty years!" says Robin.

"Yeah, Alkhatib was where I was born, but my parents got us out twenty years ago. It wasn't easy," says Ibis.

"Oh..."

The two quietly eat their sandwiches for a moment, before Robin speaks again.

"So, what do you do?" asks Robin. "I work at Arx Corporation customer service."

"You mean the people that put us on hold for thirty minutes and then try to have us buy a new product instead of fixing the one we paid for?" says Ibis.

"Yes, but that's company policy. I personally hate it, but they pay me so I can pay my bills."

Robin's phone beeps, and she grumbles, removes her gloves, pulls out her phone, and swipes away the multitude of dating app and weather notifications; the current dating app notification was from *Solar Flare* and the user was from an anonymous Black-Feathers. Robin doesn't even bother checking as she swipes it away. She puts the notifications on silent, returns her phone to her pocket, and puts on a fresh pair of plastic gloves.

"So, what do you do?" asks Robin, flashing a smile to pretend she wasn't interrupted.

"I am a photographer for Federation Systems News." For emphasis, Ibis holds up his press pass, which has a stoic photo of him, plus droopy eyes and bedraggled hair. "I had a rough week, but the next picture will be better."

"I think it's good," says Robin.

"You don't have to lie."

They eat some more.

"So, what brings you out here?" asks Robin.

"*The City of Clouds* is having an event celebrating Jay Azure's new role as captain of the habitat. I'm going to get some pictures, and–"

"There you are!" blurts a new metro-sexual voice.

Ibis and Robin turn and see a wiry man with a shiny bald head and a foundation of makeup covering his caramel-colored skin. He is also wearing shiny eye shadow, and his eyelashes are heavy on the black. His suit is a gaudy mashup of neon stripes on dark blue fabric, including his tie, which has a smirking sun pin. Behind him is a woman with pale skin, wearing an all-black suit, pitch-black sunglasses, and black hair tied into a ponytail.

The odd man's steps are bouncy with a flamboyant roll in his hips, while the woman walks like a machine. Ibis groans and looks away to finish his sandwich, and when the newcomer stops by him, he clears his throat while his female escort stays a few steps back with her hands in front of her and her eyes on Robin. This sends shivers up Robin's spine.

"Ibis, you imbecile. I told you to wait for me at 3A-I-B," he says.

Ibis, still chewing, points past the new pair, and everyone looks at the brightly lit sign that says *3A-I-B*.

The stranger looks back at Ibis, and Ibis is now sipping his drink.

"Technically you aren't there. You're here at this place," says the strange fellow.

"The horror of being fifty feet away," drones Ibis.

"I'm sorry, but who are you?" asks Robin.

"Me? You don't know who I am?" says the man.

Robin shakes her head while sipping her drink, and the stranger scoffs while the mystery woman pulls out a piece of paper and gives it to the man. The man unfolds it to show a crumpled-up, frayed award for *Best Student Journalist: Albatross High School*.

"Darling, I am only the most important and most respected journalist in this territory of the Federation of Sol Systems. That's right! You are looking at Sandy Sparrow. Number one journalist in the Prospect Sector!"

Sparrow tilts his nose up while sharply returning the paper to his escort.

She takes it, folds it quickly, and stuffs it in her coat pocket. Meanwhile, Ibis rolls his eyes and Robin stares at Sparrow blankly.

"But the award was for high school," says Robin.

"They just haven't given me my award yet because they're afraid of me," says Sparrow. "Besides, I'm important, and you're a pleb. So, what do you know about the brutality of high school journalism and the terrors beyond it? Nothing? I thought so!"

"Sparrow, relax. You don't know much about her," says Ibis.

"I know her sense of style is hideous," says Sparrow.

Robin looks at her clothes, and Sparrow claps his hands.

"But enough chit-chat, Aladdin. We have a ship to catch, and I want to make sure everything is ready for my first-class flight!" says Sparrow.

Ibis sips his drink, pushes his sandwich away, and looks at Robin apologetically. "Well, it was nice talking to you."

"Likewise," says Robin. "Maybe we'll see each other on *The City of Clouds*."

"I know we will."

Ibis leaves money on the counter, grabs his luggage, and reluctantly follows Sparrow. After the two walk past the escort, the escort points four fingers at her sunglasses, then points at Robin, and swiftly walks away. Once they are gone, Robin turns back to her food and stares ahead with a scrunched brow.

"What the heck was that about?"

Lift Off

"Row 18. Seat 4. Row 18. Seat 4. Row 18. Seat," mutters Robin.

Robin makes her way down the aisle of her designated ship. Getting on was easy enough. The worst part was waiting in line and having to relinquish her carry case to the ship crew for storage reasons. But the line was orderly, and all it took was an ID check and ticket scan to enter. Now here she is, going down the aisle of a large, bulbous ship that almost looks like an airplane from a baby toy set.

The ship has multiple aisles, is brightly lit with warm colors, and has large, comfortable seats. With the way the boarding process works, Robin does not have to worry about large amounts of people, since many are seated already, which also helps with process of elimination. Another thing that helps is that the rows and seats are clearly marked.

"Row 18. Seat 4. Row 18. Seat 4. Row 18. Seat," repeats Robin.

The person walking behind her rolls his eyes due to her slow pace, but Robin doesn't notice this. She counts the rows as she walks slowly, having with her just the clothes on her back and the phone and wallet in her pockets. When she finds her seat, she quickly sits down and takes a deep breath.

There is plenty of legroom between her and the seat in front of her and behind her, so she reclines and props up her legs. After testing the relaxation of the position, she returns the seat to its original position, and finds a TV clipped to the ceiling above her. She pulls the TV down, which leads to it turning on with a pleasant message.

"Thank you for choosing Prosperity Inter-System Travels. Viewing choices will be displayed shortly."

Robin slides the TV back in place and finds a menu tucked in the side of her seat. She opens it and finds water and soda in the double digits, stronger drinks in the triple digits, and snacks almost reaching the triple digits. She puts the menu away, and a man near her age sits next to her. She looks at him, and he ignores her.

He has fair skin, neatly combed brown hair, and hazel eyes. He is wearing casual clothes and a dark, hooded jacket that has a speeding cloud with three striking lightning bolts stitched on his shoulder. He also has a good build; not a muscular beast, but still strong enough to hold his own. The man has headphones around his neck, and a circular music player in his hand. He takes his shoes off, locks them in a basket underneath his seat, and then he buckles in, slips on his headphones, reclines his seat, and closes his eyes.

Robin awkwardly removes her shoes, and fumbles around to lock them in her basket. Once they are secure, she wrestles with the harness, and after she is secured, she reclines in her seat and tries to relax by mimicking the man next to her. Her muscles are stiff, her heart races, and her throat becomes tight. Then her eyes snap open and she puts the seat up, and after some hesitation, she awkwardly taps the man's shoulder.

At first, he doesn't respond, but when she taps him again, his eyes snap open and he looks at her. She motions him to take off his headphones, which he reluctantly does, and then he puts the chair in its normal position.

"Can I help you, miss?" he asks.

"Hi, I'm Robin Brook," says Robin.

She extends her hand while flashing an anxious smile, and he gives her an odd look as he shakes her hand.

"Bartholomew Blackbird," he says.

"Bartholomew? That's a nice name," says Robin.

"My mom thought so, too. But I prefer to be called Blackbird. It sounds cooler."

"Oh... Okay. Mr. Blackbird, I don't want to come off as weird or anything, but I've never been off the planet before. Do you have any tips for space travel?"

Blackbird thinks for a few seconds. "Inhale five seconds, exhale eight seconds is a common trick for liftoff, but for the traveling part, I like listening to music, listening to audio books, or watching movies."

"What kind of music do you listen to?" asks Robin.

Blackbird seethes. "Oh, I see what this is. You seem very nice, but I'm afraid I'm already taken."

"By a girl?"

"Yes. I am taken by someone of the female species. Her name is... Mary... Proppins."

Blackbird's brows scrunch like his brain is condemning his tongue.

"Mary Proppins?" says Robin.

"Yep. She's nice. School teacher. The good one. Not the weird ones you see on the news. Anyway, I'm going to listen to some music. When we lift off, focus on your breathing, and think about something other than fiery death or being launched out by atmospheric decompression. After we exit the atmosphere, you can listen to music, watch TV or movies, or listen to audio books through the TV."

Before Robin can say anything, Blackbird puts his headphones on, closes his eyes, and reclines in his seat. Seeing this, Robin sighs and reclines in her seat and stares at the ceiling. A few minutes pass, and a bell dings over the intercom.

"Attention everyone, this is your captain speaking," says a bored man over the speakers. *"We are due to lift off very shortly. Stewards and stewardesses will be ensuring that everyone and everything is properly secured before liftoff. Please remain seated for the duration of ascension and wait for the gravity generator to turn on before removing your harnesses. Failure to comply will result in fines and,or, probation time. Thank you for choosing Prosperity Inter-System Travels."*

The intercom clicks off, and a steward and stewardess walk by and check the harnesses on their respective sides. They give Robin's harness a tighter tug, then leave for the next row. A few minutes later, the steward and stewardess walk down to the far end of their aisle and buckle up. A few minutes later, the bell dings again and the captain's voice returns.

"Alright, passengers. Everyone and everything has been safely secured. Hang tight, keep calm, and thank you again for choosing Prosperity Inter-System

Travels."

The intercom clicks off, the interior lights dim, and the vehicle quivers as the engine rumbles. Robin closes her eyes and takes sharp breaths while her fingers hook into the arms of her chair.

Moments later, the engine's rumbling turns to whines and she feels the vehicle trudging forward. Soon it gradually turns, and it moves forward again. The engine's whining steadily turns to screaming as the vehicle's speed increases. Robin's heart thrashes in her chest, and her teeth sink into her lip while her eyes are locked shut.

The craft rattles, and Robin feels like her insides are being scrambled as the craft speeds along, tilting up and up and up and up. Robin's bones shake, and she cracks her eye open and sees Bartholomew is completely relaxed with his hands folded across his chest and his eyes closed.

Across from her, other passengers put on brave faces. Minutes pass by, and Robin feels herself lifting slightly in her seat. She fights to keep herself anchored down, and after another minute or two, there is a loud hum, and the lights turn on. With the lights comes gravity that puts her back in her seat.

"Attention, passengers. This is your captain speaking. We are now in space. Gravity is turned on, and you are now free to walk around the ship until further notice. Please remember where you are seated, and stewards and stewardesses will bring snacks and refreshments at appropriate times during the trip. Thank you for choosing Prosperity Inter-System Travels."

Robin adjusts her seat and pulls down the TV. This time, a touch-menu comes up, and she selects the music tab. She presses the Ambient/Orchestra tab, goes to Ambient, and slips on her headphones. Smooth, calming music flows into her ears, and a lush, mountainous forest fades into view. The music does miracles in relaxing Robin, but her peace is interrupted when the stewardess appears next to her and Blackbird, pushing a cart of food and drinks.

"Excuse me, would any of you like a drink or a snack?" asks the stewardess.

Blackbird pulls down his headphones. "Just water, ma'am. I have chocolate coins for a snack."

"And you, ma'am?" asks the stewardess.

"Pretzels and water please," says Robin.

The stewardess gives the pair their order, they pay a hefty bill, and she continues on her path. After that, Blackbird puts on his headphones, and Robin does the same. They listen to their music and enjoy their snacks and drinks in silence.

*****

In the first-class area, every passenger group has large seats with multiple massage and heat settings, a table with service alert buttons, and TVs that fold up next to the arm of the chair. The first-class passengers are separated from the rest of the passengers by a thick door, and there is a bar being operated by a steward currently making drinks.

In the section closest to the first-class exit door is Sparrow, his escort, and Ibis. Sparrow is reclined on his seat with his feet on the table, Ibis is sipping his water, and the escort is reading a superhero comic book with her sunglasses still on.

"Ibis, I'm going to need you to do me a favor," says Sparrow.

"Sure," says Ibis.

"Do exactly what I tell you to do. Meet me where I want to be met and be punctual. None of that nonsense down below," says Sparrow.

"No problem."

"And Raven," says Sparrow to his escort.

Raven lowers her comic book.

"Remember, you're my bodyguard, so *please* for the love of God do not run off," says Sparrow.

"Sure," says Raven, her voice insouciant.

"Oh, you do talk," teases Ibis.

"Of course I talk," says Raven Black.

"Let's stick to business. I'm going to need great pictures for my article about Jay Azure and his new position as captain of *The City of Clouds*," says Sparrow.

"There's plenty of great scenery we can use, and Bellona's colors already give the place a great tint," says Ibis.

Sparrow smiles and leans back, fully relaxed. "There's the reason why I picked you. You love photography, so you'll get me great pictures to go with my articles. Try to get a wide range, will you? I want dramatic shots, funny shots, even standard bland shots that are slightly above average."

Ibis cocks a brow. "Bland shots?"

Sparrow nods. "Yeah, you don't want to overload the visuals with too much grandeur or else you'll give your eyes diabetes. You must give people visual breaks every now and then."

Raven and Ibis stare at Sparrow's suit.

"Also, another reason why I wanted you was because I think we got off on the wrong foot on our last encounter and this cooperation can smooth things out," says Sparrow.

"You mean the hotel room thing that *you* flipped out about?" says Ibis.

"Uh... Yeah. And I'm trying to make amends."

"What hotel room?" asks Raven.

"I got his hotel room when he didn't claim it, and he's been mad ever since," says Ibis.

Raven scoffs and looks at Sparrow. "Wow. Petty much?"

"Petty? Me? No!" says Sparrow. "I didn't get that hotel because I missed my flight, which happens, you know? Understandable... Accidental... **Infringement** on purchased services."

Ibis and Raven nod.

"But what I'm mad about is that the hotel room I got in exchange for the blunder was for plebs with one hundred thread-count sheets and I had to share the space with some drugged-up lunatic on her period that stabbed me in the neck with a fork!"

Sparrow pulls down his collar to show three dots on his neck. This makes Raven and Ibis cringe.

"Ooh... That sucks," says Raven.

Sparrow puts his collar back, fuming. "Yeah, well, Ms. Stabby died by ODing on some exotic drug. So, good riddance to her. That's water under the bridge, right?"

Ibis nods. "Right. I'll make sure to get great pictures for you, too. Maybe then you'll let go of the hotel issue."

"You being here will more than make up for the mess. The tricky part is making sure I interview Jay Azure," says Sparrow.

"And I get to have fun and do all the bodyguard stuff," says Raven with a smile.

"Yeah, sure, whatever," says Sparrow. "Now, who's hungry? I'm buying."

Welcome to The City of Clouds

Planet: BELLONA

System: FURIES

Sector: PROSPECT

Date: 20-MAR-2429

"Attention, everyone. This is your captain speaking. We are nearing your destination. Please return to and remain in your seats until further notice."

The intercom clicks off, and Robin pulls off her headphones and rubs her tired eyes while pushing the TV up. The forest is replaced with a black screen, and Robin puts the headphones on a hook before grabbing her shoes.

The ship's main engine shuts off, and it drifts through the void as tiny propulsion engines guide it to the habitat. When it reaches its destination, there is a thud, and a *ding* echoes in the ship.

"Attention everyone. We have now docked. Please exit in an orderly manner and thank you for choosing Prosperity Inter-System Travels and welcome to The City of Clouds."

After the stewards and stewardesses give instruction on exiting the ship, Robin and Blackbird quietly stand up with the other passengers. They don't say anything to each other, aside from quick apologies when they accidentally bump into each other from stretching their arms. The rest of the passengers' murmur at various degrees of excitement and tiredness as they exit row by row. When it gets to Robin's row, she follows Blackbird out, and he slips on his headphones again and briskly walks down the aisle.

After Robin exits the ship, she finds herself in a tube where a habitat worker wearing a blue and white utility suit waves people down a tunnel with small lights on the roof and walls. The steps and chatter bounce off the walls, and the amount of body heat radiating from the people in the enclosed space is enough to keep the chill away. After the crowd exits the tunnel, Blackbird makes a beeline for the luggage retrieval station, and Robin paces around, dumbstruck at what she is seeing.

The new area has a curving, glass wall with a slight shimmer to it, and she can see the side of the transport ship. Beyond the ship is space, with tiny stars dotting the sky, as well as something else.

Something massive.

Robin approaches the walkway railing and stares at the planet beneath the habitat.

"Bellona," whispers Robin. She chuckles and covers her mouth to hide her grin and her body trembles with excitement. "So, that's what you look like? Those pictures don't do you justice."

The light from Bellona shines through the tinted observation window, bathing the plush furniture placed strategically around the area and Robin in a red tint.

Robin watches the swirling stripes roll over each other and glide along Bellona's rotation. Red rolls to brown, brown rolls to blue, and blue rolls to green. All the various shades of these colors add thin or thick veins in the stripes.

Currently, a red eye is looking at Robin, and it really does look like an eye with its red, ovular shape and dark red inner circle. Flashes of light streak through and wrap around the eye before disappearing soon after. Just thinking about the size of Bellona is nauseating enough, but to see the streaks of lightning really brings Robin to wonder what sort of mysticism is involved in making a planet do that.

While Robin stares at the planet, she notices out of the corner of her eye Blackbird and other passengers walking by with their luggage, so she hurries to an area where a couple of employees are. Workers retrieve the passengers' luggage, and while Robin waits, a light brown–skinned woman stands next to her with light brown eyes and straight black hair. She is wearing a wrist-top computer and wearing a long coat with simple clothing and a pair of dark purple sunglasses hanging from her shirt collar.

"Funny isn't it? This whole hurry up and wait thing, right?" says Robin awkwardly.

Robin finishes with a giggle, but the other person just shrugs.

"It's no problem. I don't have much, and my job doesn't officially start for a few days," says the stranger.

"Oh? What do you do?" asks Robin.

"I'm a safety inspector."

Robin nods, takes a deep breath, and holds out her hand. "I'm Robin. I work for Arx Corporation customer service."

"You mean like one of those people who put me on hold for thirty minutes just to up-sell me something?"

Robin drops her hand and looks down meekly. "That's company policy."

"It's a dumb policy. But I guess it's not entirely your fault." The female holds out her hand. "My name is Nightingale, by the way."

"Charmed!" Robin perks up and shakes Nightingale's hand. That is when she notices that she is next in line. "Sorry, I have to go really quick!"

"Same."

Robin goes to the employee and gives her ticket stub, and Nightingale goes to the other employee and gives her stub. After Robin gets her carry case and Nightingale gets her large backpack, they go to a kiosk manned by a habitat employee wearing a blue suit with white bands on their sleeves. Robin puts her ID and what remains of her ticket on the counter.

"Hi, I'm Robin Brook. I have a hotel room waiting for me," says Robin.

"And here's another one," grumbles the employee, his tag saying "Chick."

"Sorry?"

"Another vacation lottery winner. I wish I could get a free vacation, but *nooo*... I get to work like an ant." Chick stamps Robin's ticket with a QR code and slides it back to her. "Don't lose that or you'll be stranded here."

Robin's eyes are wide, her mouth sealed shut, and Chick gives Robin a key numbered 324. She snatches the key, quickly thanks him, and moves aside while Nightingale gets her key.

"Hello there," says Chick.

"Hello. I have a hotel room reserved," says Nightingale.

Chick stamps Nightingale's ticket. "Yep. Everyone does around here."

Chick retrieves Nightingale's key, and she glares at him, leading to his movements to suddenly be sluggish as he slides the key to her. After Nightingale gets her key, she walks by Robin and the two leave the vicinity.

Their steps are in tune as they traverse the walkway, passing map displays and small stores. Soon they come across a large domed area, with the walkway forming a ring around the lobby. At the center is a statue of a short-haired woman wearing a muscled cuirass with leather strips, shoulder and shin pads, gauntlets, a cape with a spear in one hand, and a flag with an eagle as a pole cap in the other.

The statue is all metal with nearly seamless lines from the attachments, and the only thing that isn't metal is the actual flag, which is red with a gold planet and swirling green and purple stars around it. Tourists and inhabitants alike gravitate towards it, and the main lobby area has a ring of windows, so Bellona's red light shines in with no interference.

"Oh, cool!" says Robin.

She goes to the railing to get a closer look at the statue, and notices people taking pictures of the statue as well as small shops and eateries lining the perimeter.

"We should go down there and have lunch," says Robin. She turns around and sees Nightingale walking away, and her smile drops. "Darn it…"

*****

Music flows through Bartholomew Archibald Blackbird's ears. He sees the world around him and registers just enough of it so he doesn't bump into anybody. The heavy riff of guitars, drums, and loud vocals keep his steps moving, and his hands grip his bag's straps tight while he travels through the ever-shifting maze of bodies, coming to a stop at a small, partially enclosed lobby with a few elevators.

He pushes a button to call an elevator and bobs his head to the tune of the music. The doors slide open. He steps inside and turns just in time to see Robin hurrying to the elevator with her carry case rolling behind her. He calmly sticks his foot in the sensor, thus preventing the doors from closing.

Robin gets in the elevator. She smiles anxiously at him while the doors seal, right as the worst-dressed man he had ever seen comes into view, holding his hand out and shouting something.

The door closes and Blackbird doesn't care. He looks to his side and sees Robin is saying something to him, but he can't understand her due to the music in his ears, but he gives a thumbs-up anyway.

Robin nods and smiles and leans against the wall. She talks some more, and after a short while, the elevator doors open to Residential Cloud 3. It is a brightly lit area with green bands, rows of plants under UV lights, and mist machines spraying recycled water.

As Blackbird walks down the hallway, Robin walks next to him, still talking, but doesn't notice her until she stands in front of Room 324, whereas he is at Room 326. It is at that point that Blackbird pulls off his headphones and looks at Robin critically.

"Excuse me, are you staying there?" asks Blackbird.

Robin checks her key, then the room number, and looks at Blackbird with a confused look.

"Yeah... Why?" says Robin.

"On vacation?" says Blackbird.

"Yeah..."

"Oh... Neat."

Blackbird then swiftly enters his room and closes and locks his door.

*****

Robin stares at Blackbird's door. A red light shines from a bar above the frame, and she looks at her door and scrunches her brow.

"Why don't you have friends, Robin? Everyone else has friends, Robin. Go make friends, Robin," says Robin in a mockery of Emerald's voice.

Robin enters her hotel room and closes the door. Her room is a studio-sized space where everything is out in the open with the only enclosed space being the bathroom.

The apartment also has a complimentary dwarf tree underneath a UV light band and mist projector with a note welcoming her to *The City of Clouds*.

And while the plant is nice, a thick black curtain near her bed is what piques Robin's interest. She pulls it aside and finds that the round, tinted window grants her a view of Bellona. The tint dilutes the red light, but it still gives her room a red hue.

A smile tugs on Robin's lips and a tingle runs up her spine as her eyes fixate on Bellona's eye and the lighting surging through it and its gaseous bands swirling around.

"This is cool," says Robin.

*****

Inside the elevator, Ibis stands in the corner, Sparrow is in the other corner, rubbing his brow, and Raven is standing stiff and silent in the middle. Everyone is holding their own bag, and relaxing elevator music plays over the speaker.

"You didn't have to get that upset about it," says Ibis.

"Yes, I did," says Sparrow.

"Maybe he didn't see you."

"She saw me."

"Well, still. Your reaction could have been better."

"What was wrong with my reaction?"

Ibis arches a brow.

((((O))))

"No! No! No! Don't you dare!" yelled Sparrow as he bolted towards the elevator.

The fashion model–looking woman was staring right at him, grinning like a demon from ear to ear when the elevator doors clicked shut with a pleasant ding and Sparrow slammed right into it.

"Are you kidding me!? Fuck you, you petty bitch! I know you remember me!"
screamed Sparrow.

Sparrow punched the elevator door, and then he kicked it, and then he went over
to a garbage can and threw it across the hallway, knocking over a potted plant.

((((O))))

Ibis and Sparrow stare at each other for a few more seconds before Sparrow
looks away.

"I don't see what the big deal is," says Sparrow.

"If you get a ticket, then you have only yourself to blame," says Ibis.

"I'm not going to get a ticket. I'm too important."

"Really?" asks Raven.

"Yes. Really. I'm well respected in certain circles," says Sparrow.

"Then why are you making me carry around your high school journalism
award?"

"Because it's sentimental!" snaps Sparrow. He takes a deep breath.
"Besides, how many award-winning high school journalists do you know?"

"Six," says Ibis flatly.

"There was Gary..." Raven snaps her fingers many times. "Gary... Gary..."

"Okay, I don't care," says Sparrow.

"Gary Salamiin! Yes! Gary Salamiin!" says Raven excitedly.

She giggles, and Ibis and Sparrow stare at her with curiosity for the former
and annoyance for the latter.

"Gary is the reason why I have a criminal record. He ratted me out to the
police after I rigged the school toilets to explode from flushing... And sprayed
poison ivy juice on the toilet paper in the men's room. That was a long time
in juvie," says Raven.

Sparrow looks at Ibis. "This is why I hate women. They're monsters."

The elevator stops, the doors slide open, and the entourage steps out into
a brightly lit hallway, with colorful lights and holographic projections of
beautiful people enjoying fine food and dances and a curved glass wall showing
Bellona.

"Well, let's get this rolling. The quicker we do the introductions, the quicker we can get our jobs done," says Sparrow.

The group walks down the hall, and Ibis looks at Bellona's eye, hating how it feels like it is following him. He shakes away the feeling and puts his attention back to Sparrow. When they reach a large, round door guarded by four security officers, Sparrow smiles at them.

"Hello, there! Can you tell Jay Azure that Sandy Sparrow, Ibis Ajam, and Raven Black are here," says Sparrow.

The security guard pushes a button on the wall next to the door.

"Sir, we have a Sandy Sparrow, Ibis Ajam, and Raven Black here to see you," says the guard.

"Check their IDs. If they're real, let them in. If they're decievers shoot them down to Bellona," says a grizzled voice through the speaker.

The intercom clicks off and the security guard pulls out a scanner.

"Alright, let's see the IDs," says the guard.

Everyone gives their IDs to the guard, the scans turn up positive, and the guard punches in the security code on the door. The door slides open after a series of hisses and clicks, revealing a penthouse with two long, curved windows. One gives an excellent view of Bellona, and the other has an unobstructed view of the expanse of space. They can see Alecto, too. It is not big, but it is the brightest dot in the black void.

The penthouse has fancy furniture, expensive and high thread-count sheets, and an aquarium with colorful fish swimming in it, plus a small orchard of dwarf fruit trees hooked to an irrigation system. Lights stretch across the ceiling and swirl around in a replica of the Milky Way Galaxy, including one large light in the middle.

The guards in the room are all wearing armored vests and pads, their weapons are out in the open, and they have zip-cuffs on their belts.

Then there is Jay Azure.

Ibis's steps have slowed by a fraction and his eyes focus on the old man. He is smiling with pearly white teeth, thick white hair, and a casual suit that covers his heavy, muscular build. Jay walks over to Sparrow with his hand outstretched, and Sparrow goes to him. The two shake hands, and when they step back, Jay looks at Ibis.

"I know you, Ibis Ajam. You took fantastic pictures at the Old Arabia Expo," says Jay.

Ibis smiles thinly. "Thank you. It was an honor to be there."

"I'm sorry I couldn't be there to give you your award, but this system is loaded with resources. Lots of mining contracts, lots of new mines, expansions of old ones. Overall, there is phenomenal potential for great wealth and other things from this system and the Sector as a whole. Who knows? A few more years and we might have the resources to reclaim Greater Arabia," says Jay.

"One can hope," says Ibis.

Sparrow is frowning at that point, but he switches it to a thin smile when Jay and Ibis look at him.

"Why the long face?" asks Jay.

"Long flight. The boss at the headquarters just wanted me to meet you before we got settled in," says Sparrow.

"Long flight or still grouchy nobody's given you an award for your shitty articles?"

Sparrow forces a chuckle. "Well, its hard work being a journalist."

"Everything is hard work." Jay looks at Raven. "And you, Raven, I looked you up. You have a criminal record. Time in juvie for very bad pranks."

Raven shrugs. "April Fool's Day can get pretty wicked."

Jay chuckles and pats Raven's shoulder. "I like you already. Though, I don't know why Sparrow hired you to be a bodyguard."

"He wants me to protect him from pirates," says Raven.

"We cannot deny that the pirate attacks have gotten worse. But still, you're not bodyguard material, and there's a lot of guards here. Maybe you're just eye candy?"

"As long as I'm getting paid, I don't care," replies Raven.

"You should care."

Raven's lip twitches, and suddenly, the door opens and a middle-aged man with dyed red hair enters. Jay immediately smiles when he sees him and waves him over. Sparrow intently watches the newcomer approach while Ibis and

Raven smile politely at him.

"There you are! Come on over!" says Jay.

The man has a skip in his step as he approaches the group, and he and Jay shake hands while Jay looks at Sparrow's group.

"Do you know who this guy is?" asks Jay.

"No," says Ibis.

"Nope," says Raven.

"Vaguely familiar," says Sparrow.

"This is Dunlin Feathers. He runs the vacation lottery," says Jay. "He also vouched for me when I was running for captain of this tin can. Dunlin, these people are from the newspaper, so I want you to personally take them to the best rooms we have. Sparrow is going to be interviewing me later, and Ibis is going to be taking a lot of pictures."

Dunlin shakes Sparrow's hand. "I'm a big fan of your work."

"Finally! Someone appreciates me," says Sparrow with a laugh. "If only more people were like you."

"Yeah, if only. And what's her deal?" asks Dunlin, nodding to Raven.

"I'm his bodyguard," says Raven.

"Is that right?"

Sparrow and Raven nod, and Dunlin grins.

"Well, you won't have to worry about a thing. We've got a lot of fine officers who will keep you safe from any excitement," says Dunlin. "Anyway, let's get you settled in before thee day runs us ragged."

*****

Robin stares at Bellona's eye with an odd smile. Her eyes trace the swirling clouds in the eye but snap to the lightning when it zips across the gas giant's storm. She has no idea how long she was staring at it before she checks the time. Seeing that time flew way too fast, she slaps her watch shut and leaps to her feet.

"Lunch. I need lunch," says Robin.

She hurries to the bathroom and checks herself in the mirror. She removes her finger-less cloves to quickly wash her face. Then she brushes her hair, makes sure her clothing has no wrinkles, and polishes the buttons on her vest and jacket. Once done, she slips on her gloves and hurries out the door.

It doesn't take long for her to get to a Klumsy K's in the habitat's main area. *The City of Clouds* layout is very convenient, with lots of interconnected pathways, walkways, and elevators to join the various pods (or "clouds" as they like to say).

"Table for one, miss?" asks an approaching host as Robin catches her breath in the doorway.

"Yes, please," says Robin.

The host grabs a menu and rolled-up silverware, and takes Robin to the bar. When she sits down, the server sets down her silverware and menu, and leaves to assist another customer. Soon after, a waiter appears: blonde hair, blue eyes, good build. This immediately gets Robin's attention, but all hope is dashed when she sees the wedding ring.

"Welcome to Klumsy K's. I'm Joe. I'll be your server," he says.

"Hi, Joe. I'll need just a moment," says Robin. "But a water to drink will be a nice start."

"Certainly."

Joe leaves, and then Blackbird sits next to her with a menu and silverware being placed in front of him. This brings a confused frown to Robin.

"What are you doing here?" asks Robin.

"I was going to have lunch, and I saw you here alone. So, here I am," says Blackbird.

Joe returns with a water, and Blackbird politely asks for a cherry soda. After Joe leaves, Robin pulls out plastic gloves to put over her finger-less gloves.

"Don't you have a girlfriend? Mary Proppins?" asks Robin.

"No. I lied," says Blackbird.

"How do I know you're lying about lying?"

"Why would I lie about lying?"

"Well, you apparently lied about Mary Proppins."

"That was one time, and I was nervous. And I was nervous because I think I know you. Now, if I'm wrong, just say so, but if I'm right... Hold on, let me check the menu first."

Robin's throat clenches and her whole body tightens. All she can think about is the criminal she accidentally killed. His broken and charred body getting run over, and all the publicity and the stench of electric fire, cooked flesh, and heavy rain.

Joe returns with the cherry soda and sets it in front of Blackbird.

Blackbird thanks him, but even though his tone is not threatening, Robin's heart is racing. Her mind is clouded with words and screams to run, but her legs keep her in place, and her lungs are determined to hold her air in.

Robin watches her soon-to-be killer flip through his menu. After he's done, he looks at Robin with an intense fire in his eyes and face red from embarrassment.

"Are you Chickadee_01 from Dating Universe?" asks Blackbird.

Robin's thoughts dissolve instantly, her phone buzzes from notifications, and her eyes bulge. The two are quiet for a few more seconds, before Robin's brain decides to work again.

"Who are you?" asks Robin.

"DynamicDomino4D4. I sent you a friend request if you are Chickadee_01. If you aren't, don't worry about it and pretend I didn't say anything," says Blackbird.

Robin looks down, eyes darting side to side, as if reading a page on the bar. Then she looks at Blackbird with a small sneer.

"You're from Venus. I turned you down because you're all the way on Venus! I told the app just the Furies System, but it keeps doing that to me!" Robin groans and rubs her face. "Oh, my goodness, why is that app so stupid?"

"You also never answered my message," says Blackbird.

"Because you live all the way on Venus! And I was out of free monthly credits," says Robin.

"Yeah, I use the free monthly credits, too. Dating apps are basically highway robbery. I don't know why I use them," says Blackbird.

"Me neither. But that's not the point! Why are you even all the way over here? The Sol System has habitats to vacation on, right?"

"Yeah, but I won a vacation lottery for this place, and I just got a sign-on bonus for joining the Strike Craft Force, so I'm enjoying my last bit of freedom before reporting to Ganymede."

Robin's eye twitches, and Joe returns, smiling patiently.

"Are you two ready to order?" asks Joe.

"Classic burger all the way. Seasoned fries," says Blackbird. "I'll pay for her meal, too."

Robin strains a smile. "Thanks... I'll have a chicken salad please, with lots of ranch and croutons."

Joe writes down the order, thanks them, and leaves. After he is gone, Robin and Blackbird look at each other.

"Are you stalking me?" asks Robin.

"No," says Blackbird.

"It's just weird how all this is lining up... How you got a vacation lottery, and I got a vacation lottery, our rooms are next to each other, and we're on the same dating app."

Blackbird shrugs. "Yeah, that's weird, but as the saying goes; 'It's a small galaxy, after all.'" He reaches into his jacket pocket, pulls out a chocolate coin, and offers it to Robin. "Chocolate?"

Robin stares at it for a few seconds, then she snatches it and moodily eats it. This makes Blackbird chuckle.

"What?" says Robin.

"You need to relax. This is vacation time, remember?" says Blackbird.

"Well, no offense, but I find you weird, and everything about our encounter's weird."

"But not weird enough for you to reject chocolate?"

Robin grunts, and Joe returns with their food. They thank him, and Joe puts the receipt with Blackbird. They eat in silence for a few minutes, until Robin awkwardly speaks.

"Thank you for paying for my meal," says Robin.

"You're welcome. And I just want to say that while things won't work between us because of distance, I still think we're going to have a good time on this ship," says Blackbird.

"You think so?"

"Well, maybe not as good as I'd like, but we're vacation neighbors, so might as well make some good memories while we're here."

"True..."

Blackbird tilts his glass to Robin. "Cheers for an okay time?"

Robin taps her glass against his. "Cheers... Weirdo."

*****

Inside a dimly lit room, Nightingale is sitting on the floor with her wrist-top plugged into a terminal. The glow of her wrist-top shines on her face, reflecting off her skin and eyes. Her fingers quickly tap the buttons, and on her screen are two feeds. One is a looped recording of the camera, and the other is schematics of *The City of Clouds*, currently being downloaded.

After it downloads, Nightingale pulls up another window and swiftly types and sends an email.

* * *

To: *Love*

From: *Lover*

Subject: *[None]*

Dear Love,

Attached is what you want. The contractor was right. We're going to hit the jackpot!

Love,

Lover <3

File: *blank.zip*

* * *

After the email is sent, Nightingale puts the loop at an end-timer for five minutes, shuts down her wrist-top, and leaves with a skip in her step.

A lovely day and a lot of money are on their way.

March 24th

Today is March 24th, the day that Jay Azure is sworn in as captain of *The City of Clouds*, and Robin does not care. She wants to do something other than see a politician boost their ego, but she has found that the habitat is what most would call **boring.**

For the past few days, Robin has been walking around. All she has found are walkway tubes, leading to habitat clouds where people lived or worked, or studied, but even then, a lot of them were off-limits, due to them being habitat crew only.

As for the rest of the habitat, the scenery is nice, but there are only so many times one can stare out the window to look at black matter and glittering dots. Really, the best part of the exterior scenery is Bellona. And one of the best spots for the interior is the statue dedicated to her in the commons. There are also a few arcades scattered about, a holo-theater, a movie theater, and a gym. But these things are not enough to justify living in a constant state of boredom.

In fact, the whole vacation has been boring, and today really takes the cake. Not even the celebration of Jay Azure's victory is enough to spur Robin's excitement. People walking by her and seeing her head resting on a table and staring at Bellona's gaseous bands do not care that she is about to fall into a boredom-induced coma.

Then, someone shakes her shoulder.

"Hey, you alive?" says Blackbird.

Robin's eyes shift stiffly and she sees Blackbird staring at her curiously with his headphones around his neck and music playing from the little speakers.

Behind him, security guards move around, some more sluggish than others, and habitat staff hurry to set up party tables.

Blackbird waves in front of Robin's eyes. "Hello?"

Robin blinks and sits up, her cheek red and her eyes glazed. She blinks again and looks around.

"Are you okay?" asks Blackbird.

"I'm bored," says Robin.

"Oh... Have you tried to do anything fun?"

"Like what?"

"The holo-theater? The movie theater? The arcades? The gym?"

"No."

Blackbird sits across from her. "Why not?"

"I don't feel like it."

"Ah. Boredom paradox."

"What?"

"Boredom paradox. You're in a situation that is not interesting, therefore you think about how not interesting it is, and because you're thinking about how not interesting your situation is, you become more bored because your thinking is fueling your boredom. All you gotta do to stop being bored is stop thinking about how bored you are."

"Is that you why listen to music all the time?"

Blackbird laughs. "No. I listen to music so that I don't have to think about how I relate to Oliver Twist a little too much. Only, instead of an orphanage rub by a crabby old lady, we got an orphanage run by a demented dentist."

"I'm sorry, but what is Oliver Twist?"

"It's the myth. You never heard of Oliver Twist?"

Robin shakes her head.

"Alrighty then. Maybe they'll have it at the library," says Blackbird.

"There's no library on this habitat," says Robin.

"Really?"

Robin nods.

"Well, that's dumb," says Blackbird.

"Excuse me!" calls Ibis.

Blackbird and Robin look up, and Robin smiles when she sees Ibis in front of them. He is holding his camera and staring at them with an uneasy smile.

"Ibis! Hi, how are you?" says Robin.

"I'm fine. I'm just doing some work for Sparrow," says Ibis.

The three look across the commons and see Sparrow interviewing a tired security officer while Raven eats a slice of cake from a paper plate. After a few seconds of observation, the three look back at each other.

"Anyway, I noticed you two had a good spot with Bellona behind you, and I was wondering if I could get some pictures?" says Ibis.

"That'll be fine," says Robin.

Robin rests her red cheek on her hand to hide the impurity, and Blackbird adjusts himself, so he is looking directly at the camera. Both smile, and Ibis takes a rapid stream of pictures. While he's doing this, Jay Azure approaches with Dunlin, and an old, short, and fat black woman wearing a chef's outfit.

"There's my favorite photographer!" says Jay. He slaps Ibis on the shoulder, making him stumble a bit. "Hey, I want some pictures with me and my two favorite people on this ship. You've already met Dunlin, but this fine young lady is Mavis Beak. She's in charge of the food safety and planned all the food for the celebration of my victory!"

"Oh, pleasure to meet you, ma'am," says Ibis.

Ibis and Mavis shake hands, despite Mavis looking like she wants to be somewhere else. Before they can get set up, Jay notices Robin and Blackbird staring at him in disbelief. Which is understandable, since it is not often one comes across a trillionaire and a captain of a habitat.

"Hi there. Are you two residents of *The City of Clouds*?" asks Jay.

"We won the vacation lottery," says Blackbird.

Jay chuckles and looks at Dunlin. "Would you look at that. Two lottery winners. Sounds like you goofed a bit."

Dunlin's lips twitch to force a smile, and Jay waves him forward to the table.

"I have an idea. How about we get a group picture? Me, the captain, and Dunlin Feathers, the lottery overseer, with an anomaly of **two** winners," says Jay.

Jay sits down next to Robin, and Dunlin sits next to Blackbird. After they are seated, Jay grins brightly at Ibis. Robin and Blackbird smile normally, and Dunlin keeps a thin smile.

"Make sure you make me look like a good person," says Jay lightly as he puts his arm around Robin's shoulder. "Smile for the camera, everyone."

Everyone holds their smiles, and Ibis takes a rapid stream of pictures. When he is done, Jay turns to Robin, completely ignoring Blackbird.

"By the way, I think I know you from somewhere," says Jay.

"Oh...?" says Robin uneasily.

"Yeah, you're that chick from the news that brutally killed that robber!"

Robin pales with tears forming in her wide eyes, and Blackbird and Dunlin look at Robin with surprise.

"Seriously? You killed someone?" says Blackbird.

"It was an accident!" cries Robin.

"Okay, I'm sorry, I didn't realize you would cry. Let's start over," says Jay. "Are you Chickadee_02 from *Star Crossed*? Because I am Grandpanator1000."

Robin groans and rubs her face, with her elbows propped on the table. "Oh God, not you, too."

Jay grins. "So, you are? Great! I'm single, you're single, let's mingle."

Robin keeps her face buried. "I'd rather not."

"Can I bribe you to mingle with me?"

"Hey, she's not interested," says Blackbird sternly.

Jay looks at Blackbird with an amused smirk.

"Trust me, she is. She's just playing hard to get. It's a classic test that females pull," says Jay.

Robin gets up and leaves in a hurry, wiping tears from her eyes, and Jay waves after her.

"Call me!" yells Jay.

When Robin rounds the corner, Blackbird gets up and hurries after her, and Jay looks at Ibis and Dunlin.

"People these days," says Jay.

Ibis nods, pretending to sympathize, and Dunlin stands up.

"Well, I need to go and check the system to see why we had two winners," says Dunlin.

"Can't it wait until after the party?" asks Jay.

Dunlin shakes his head. "I'd rather not wait."

Jay shrugs. "Alright, suit yourself."

Dunlin offers a quick wave and hurries off. When he disappears into the crowd, Jay waves Mavis over.

"Mavis, I forgot you were here! Have a seat so we can get some pictures," says Jay.

Mavis strains a smile and sits next to Jay, and Ibis takes their pictures.

*****

Nearby, Sparrow and Raven are watching Ibis take pictures of Jay and Mavis. When he is done, Jay shoos Mavis away, grabs random people, and has Ibis take pictures of them.

Sparrow's lips hook to a frown with his vein throbbing on his forehead, and he shakes his head slowly. All while Raven enjoys a slice of strawberry cake.

"This is a good cake. Do you want me to get you a slice of cake?" asks Raven.

"No," says Sparrow. "I want to interview Jay Azure, so I can have materials to work with."

"Just ignore him and keep interviewing other people, like what you've been doing for the past two hours," says Raven.

"I don't like interviewing plebs."

Raven chokes on her food. "Wow. Okay. It's not their fault they were born as plebs."

"True, but them being obnoxious, inconsiderate pricks is something they have full control over, and they don't want to change. They like being menaces to society and it makes me angry."

Raven slows down her chewing, stares at Sparrow for a few seconds, and then she shakes her head and looks away.

"I think I'm going to go somewhere else for a bit," says Raven.

"Where?" asks Sparrow, his eyes still on Jay.

"Maybe an arcade or something."

"But you're my bodyguard."

"You'll be fine."

Sparrow yanks Raven's cake from her hand and starts eating it. "Fine. Whatever. Go have fun. Just remember your job and don't leave me hanging, or else you won't get paid."

Raven rolls her eyes, grabs a cup of punch off the drink table, and walks away. As she leaves, Sparrow shakes his head slowly and keeps staring at Jay and Ibis.

*****

Meanwhile, in a dark corner of *The City of Clouds*, far from prying eyes, Nightingale furiously types on her wrist-top computer. She has once again put the camera feed in her section on loop, but now she has another window open.

This one is for a dock. The camera feed has workers going about their business, but it is also on loop, so security doesn't notice what is coming next. However, her friends will have to act fast to make sure that no one is able to escape when they arrive. No amount of camera looping will stop loose lips.

She also has two more windows open. One is for a camera view of the communications room. The workers inside are scrambling, as all the screens have error messages. The other camera feed is aimed at a vault with a group of four guards sitting at a table, playing the card game War.

With the cameras on loop, and knowing that her boss is close, Nightingale sends out an email.

* * *

To: Love
From: Lover
Subject: [None]

Go.

A Murder of Pirates

Out in the airless, cold blackness, a large ship glides towards *The City of Clouds*. Its bulbous hull is blue with white stripes, and various tube-like bulges run along its length. Red lights blink on the ship, and puffs of exhaust are ejected from its sides as it approaches the lowest pod. Its exhaust ports gradually turn the ship to connect it to a tube that is extending to it. After a few minutes, the blue ship is locked to the tube with a series of hisses and clicks.

*****

Inside *The City of Clouds*, workers wearing thick yellow clothes, red gloves, and hats wait by a massive door. Swirling emergency lights swipe along the walls and floor, and when the door opens, a large, dark-skinned man wearing a similar outfit to them steps out, holding a pad in one hand and squeezing a stress ball in another. He is smiling brightly, despite the frost on his face.

"Evening, gentlemen. I got some ice from Rebecca the Ice Queen," he says.

"Right on time. The celebration is going to take a lot of water," says the lead worker. "Drinks, baking, cleaning, stuff like that."

"Wouldn't doubt it. Sign here for me."

The delivery man gives the worker the pad while large, mechanized carts with huge blocks of ice strapped on them carefully make their way out of the tunnel. After the pad is signed, the delivery man stuffs it in a zipped pocket and thanks the worker. Then reaches behind his back, pulls out a pistol, and aims it at the worker's head. The worker stops, his eyes widen, and he pales as he opens his mouth.

"Don't," orders the delivery man.

The worker clamps his mouth shut.

"You scream. You die. Clear?" says the delivery man.

The worker nods, and the others freeze and stare at the scene in total shock. Then, they put their hands up and back away when a steady stream of pirates come out of the tunnel, wearing the thick clothes and armed with rifles, shotguns, and sub machine guns. The pirates spread out, and the ones that stayed with the delivery man herd the workers to their section's lobby and have them remove the thick clothing, so they are in their white shirts and blue pants.

"Nobody panic," says the delivery man. "We're going to make this quick, so there's no misunderstandings of what we're here to do."

The other pirates return, ushering in more workers at gunpoint. Every worker is swiftly cuffed and gagged, and a large, muscular Latino pirate with gold eye shadow and golden, tribal bird tattoos covering his neck, head, and shoulders gives an automatic rifle to the delivery man.

"Thank you, Oro," says the delivery man.

The pirate, Oro A. Guila, nods, and steps back while drawing a pistol. The delivery man aims and shoots the nearest hostage through the back of the head.

The other pirates follow suit, and very quickly, the muffled screams are vanquished, and the floor, walls, and furniture are soaked in blood. The pirates shoot more rounds into the bodies, and even more into ones that are twitching. When they are done, the delivery man takes off his hat to free his braided hair, pulls off his facial hair to reveal feathers tattooed on his dark face, and he smiles at the room of corpses.

"Good shooting, everybody. Now let's get to work," says Crow Magnolia.

*****

In the bridge of *The City of Clouds*, Jay Azure looks at the ring of computer monitors, operated by personnel who appear weary. On a normal day, it would disgust him that people would be wanting to sleep on the job, but today is not a normal day. *Everyone* on the bridge looks like they are about to collapse, from computer operators to the security team.

Even the guy whose work area is a pigsty of candy and pastry wrappers should be wide awake from all the sugar consumption is drowsy and knocks over a can of *Extra Strength & Length Bug Killer Spray*.

"Give me a bottle of water," orders Jay to the nearest guard on his personal detail.

The guard leaves, and Jay looks at one of the monitors. After staring at it for a moment, he scrunches his brow and approaches it.

The sluggish worker suddenly jerks and sits upright when he realizes Jay is next to him. Jay leans over him and continues to stare at the monitor, and he notices a faint glitch in the feed. He waits another minute, and when the glitch returns at exactly sixty seconds, he steps away and goes to one of his guards, right as the other one returns with a bottle of water.

"Let's go back to my suite," says Jay.

"But the celebration party, sir," says the guard.

Jay takes the bottle, opens it, and sniffs it. Then he takes a sip and analyzes the taste. It tastes like water, so he swallows it, seals it, and quickly walks to the exit.

"Forget the celebration. We're going to be having a different party very soon," says Jay.

*****

Robin briskly walks along the edge of the commons area, eyes red and puffy. Her hands tremble as she holds her arms, and she ignores everyone around her. The statue of Bellona is always in her peripheral vision, but her wet eyes are staring ahead, while her brain tries to think of where to go to distract herself from the memory of killing the criminal. But *The City of Clouds* is so boring that she knows she'll end up staring off into space; but with the curse of memory to occupy her mind instead of boredom.

"Robin!" calls Blackbird.

Robin tries to ignore him, but when he ends up next to her, his headphones still playing music, and she can't help but glance at him.

"Robin are you okay?" asks Blackbird.

"No, and I don't want to talk about it," says Robin.

"I understand." Blackbird moves in front of her, and she stops and looks at him when he puts his hands on her shoulders. "But I'd like to try to take your mind off of whatever terrible thing you're thinking about."

"Good luck. I've been trying to forget it for a year, and nothing works," says Robin.

"What if I take you to the holo-theater?"

"The holo-theater sucks."

Blackbird's mouth clamps with a strained hum, and Robin looks down.

"I'm sorry, but I really want to be alone, right now," she says apologetically. "I'll just go back to my hotel and watch reruns of whatever is on TV."

Blackbird nods. "Okay... Can I at least walk with you?"

Robin hesitates, looks at him, and right as she is about to nod, Raven comes barreling through out of nowhere and bumps into Blackbird, spilling a cup of fruit punch all over his jacket. Robin is lucky enough to have the reflexes to step back before the cursed liquid gets on her clothes. All three pause and stare at the wet mess that drips off the jacket sleeve and stains the carpet.

"Oh... Wow. My bad," says Raven. Then she notices Robin. "Hold on, I know you. You were at the launch port, right? Yeah! You were trying to seduce our photographer with your harlot ways and make us late for our flight!"

Robin's jaw drops. "What? No! Why would you even think that? We were having lunch! *And* we were two hours early, as per recommendation by the Federation Interstellar Travel Agency."

"Oh, look at you go. Freaking nerd."

Robin glares at Raven, and Blackbird is studying the mess on his jacket, muttering to himself. When he looks at Raven to scold her, something in his brain clicks, and he narrows his eyes.

"Wait a minute. Do I know you?" asks Blackbird.

Raven stares at him, and Robin stares at Raven curiously while Blackbird is intense. Raven's eyes betray the gears working in her brain, and when the information is done processing, she shakes her head.

"Nope. You must be mistaking me for someone else," says Raven.

Blackbird wags his finger at her. "No, I know you from somewhere."

Raven's face contorts to an obnoxious scoff. "Uh, no you don't. Not at all. Not even close to knowing me from somewhere."

Robin looks between the two before pointing at Raven with her thumb, while looking at Blackbird.

"Is she your ex?" asks Robin.

"No! ... She... She's the one that laced the men's bathroom toilet paper with poison ivy for April Fool's!" says Blackbird.

"Oh, the nerve of such lies!" says Raven in the least convincing way possible. "In fact, I should have you know, I've never even been to a high school. I dropped out in fifth grade, because school is for losers!"

"Yes, it was you! I ratted you out to the cops when Gary found out and told me!" says Blackbird.

"That was you!?" says Raven.

Blackbird smirks. "Knew it."

"I mean, I don't know what you're talking about."

Robin gets between the two and gently guides Blackbird away from Raven while a small crowd stares at them, snickering and taking videos.

"Okay, maybe we should calm down," says Robin. "Let's not get internet famous over stupid stuff."

"Party pooper!" shouts a random person in the crowd.

"Having poison ivy juice up my butt crack was hell!" says Blackbird, pointing at Raven.

"What are you going to do about it? Fight me! You wouldn't hit a girl, would you?" says Raven.

Blackbird's face strains and he balls his fist. "I believe in equal opportunity violence."

Raven walks backwards and flips him off. "Oh, well, I'd love to fight, but some of us have jobs to do!"

"Yeah, you do your job being Satan's bitch!"

And then Raven hurries off, leaving Robin to stare at her curiously and Blackbird to grumble and snatch party napkins to wipe away the spilled punch on his jacket. The small crowd disperses, grumbling in disappointment or still snickering.

Blackbird's method of cleaning doesn't work, and he sighs heavily and aggressively throws the torn napkins in a nearby trash can.

"Man, and this is my lucky jacket, too," says Blackbird. He looks over his shoulder and watches Raven dip into a stairwell. "And sorry about that. That Raven girl is just a real piece of shit."

Robin tugs him away and forces him to keep walking by holding his arm tight.

"Don't worry about her. Why don't you tell me about your lucky jacket?" says Robin.

Blackbird inspects his jacket with a newly found, small, proud smile. "This thing? Yeah, long story short, I got re-adopted to a better family after finding this jacket. The previous guy was a real piece of work; looked like a bull terrier and had us do crimes and shit. But anyway. a lot of other good things happened when I started wearing this jacket after I got out of juvie. Most recently, winning the vacation lottery and getting a chance to impress a dating app girl that rejected me."

"You were lucky, except for today."

"Yeah... Unless I say the jacket shielded my nice shirt from a fruit punch staining... Yeah, I'll go with that, so that way it keeps its lucky title. But I'm still going to wash this off as best as I can."

Robin nods and looks around, spotting a bench not too far from her. "Okay, I'll wait for you over there. Maybe we can watch reruns together in my hotel or something? I don't know."

Blackbird smiles. "Is that a date?"

Robin slowly shrugs. "I guess? ... Yes?"

"Awesome. I'll be back."

And with that, Blackbird hurries away. Robin sits on the bench and makes a deep, long sigh while a security guard struggling to breath leans against the pillar near her.

*****

Blackbird enters the public bathroom and hurries to the sink and soap dispenser. He squirts out a glob of soap and furiously rubs it on his jacket sleeve until it is a lather. Next he wets a paper towel and scrubs his sleeve with it until it is a shredded mess of paper towel and soap suds. Rinse and repeat.

"Freaking Raven. I hate her so much," mutters Blackbird, scrubbing faster and harder. "But I can't focus on her right now because I got permission to make a sad girl happy, so I'm going to make her happy and not worry about the other person, because if I do, I'll mess up and..."

Blackbird slows down the scrubbing, and eventually pauses and squints at the mirror in front of him. In the reflection he sees a pair of boots and security uniform pants laying on the floor. He turns around and looks at the stall they're in. He cautiously approaches it and knocks on the door.

"Hey... Are you okay?" asks Blackbird.

Silence.

He knocks again, and when there is no response, Blackbird forces the door open and finds a security guard slumped against the wall by the toilet, face blue and eyes dim.

"Oh shit," says Blackbird.

Then he hears screaming.

*****

Robin takes another deep breath and runs her shaky fingers through her hair. She glances to the side where she sees a security guard slouching next to the trash can, like a discarded doll. Robin stares at the limp guard, and then someone shrieks in the distance. There are more screams, as more guards collapse.

Robin looks at the guard again and sees his suffocated face, and she gasps and backpedals, tripping over herself. She scurries until her back hits a support pillar. She covers her mouth with tears streaking down her cheeks while people run away, trampling each other, and knocking tables and food over, spreading trash and sending balloons loose during the chaos.

*****

Jay goes into his suite, and a pair of guards seal the door while others check their weapons. While that happens, Jay goes to a wall, types in a code, and it splits open to reveal numerous monitors with various angles on the habitat. He can see the chaos of the civilians trampling each other, guards lying dead, and a swarm of heavily armed pirates going through elevators, leaving dead guards and workers behind.

"Damn pirates," growls Jay. He turns to the guards in his room. "Nobody opens that door for any reason."

"Sir, what about your vault?" asks one of his guards.

"Let them have it. We're staying here."

*****

Nightingale and a group of four pirates travel quickly down a hallway. One of the pirates is carrying a large pack, and the others are armed with rifles. They reach a sealed door, and Nightingale plugs her wrist-top computer into a terminal, types in a few commands, and the door slides open.

Beyond the door is the security detail, lying dead on the floor, all suffocated with half eaten food on the table. There is another door made of heavy bars, and the security behind that door are slumped on the table, also having half eaten food nearby. Behind them is the vault.

Nightingale hacks open the barred door, and the pirates rush to the vault and unpack a drilling machine on a tripod stand. The other pirates stand guard while Nightingale brings up schematics to the vault, and the drill operator adjusts his device according to her instructions.

Once the drill is lined up, it is bolted to the floor, and the pirate prepares it while Nightingale puts a communicator on her shoulder. She has it fully set up by the time the drill is ready, and she holds up her finger, thus halting the pirates. Then she turns on her communicator, bringing up a holographic projection of an audio box.

"Love, the vault is secured, and the drill is ready," says Nightingale.

"Good job. Now get to work. The faster we get the money, the faster we can get out of here," says Crow.

"Of course." Nightingale hangs up and looks at the driller. "Start drilling, Talon, and be careful. There's ten defense poles we need to sever without any mistakes."

Talon nods and begins his work.

*****

A service elevator dings and slides open, and Crow Magnolia steps out, armed with an automatic rifle, a pistol, and a knife. He is wearing just a vest over his torso, but he kept the thick pants. This exposes his large muscles and the various tattoos of crows, reapers, and tally marks. On his back is a tattoo of a crow with its wings expanded and its beak piercing a skull. He keeps his rifle propped against his shoulder, while his free hand squeezes his stress ball.

The large group of pirates behind him are also wearing vests, and they fan out in a quick, professional manner, sweeping the area and carefully stepping over the dead security and dragging civilians to the shops in the commons. As they do this, other pirates come out of elevators and assist in securing the commons. While they do this, Crow stops and looks up at the Bellona statue, whistling impressively.

"Nice. If she were real, she'd be a ten-ten, you know what I mean?" says Crow.

Some pirates verbally acknowledge Crow, and garbage crunches underneath his feet as he walks across the commons area. He smirks as they pass a picture declaring Jay Azure the winner of the election. They continue with speed up the stairs, snatching more civilians in that area crouching behind benches or garbage cans, or peeking out from the hallways.

During this, Crow grabs Oro and brings him close to his side.

"Grab some of our peeps and get rid of our three amigos, will you?" says Crow.

Oro nods and jogs away, grabbing other pirates and barking out orders. Most of the remaining pirates keep herding civilians into shops or eateries, but Crow's group of pirates make haste to the habitat bridge.

After reaching the locked door guarding the bridge, one of the pirates plants explosive bricks on its sides and makes an "X" of more explosives in the center. The pirates stand back a safe distance and detonate the bricks. Balls of fire and hot air spread out, shattering the glass panels for the walkway and burning the carpet.

The metal door falls over as a twisted mess, and the pirates rush in with their weapons raised. Inside, they find all the crew and the security dead, and Crow chuckles and pushes a corpse off a chair.

"My man really pulled through," says Crow.

Crow goes to the back, where there is an elevated seat inside a half ring of terminals with Jay Azure's name on a plaque, and he sits in the chair while his pirates move the bodies to a pile. As they work, Crow pulls out an instruction's manual from a drawer, props his feet on the desk, and flips through it.

After he finds what he wants, he types in some commands, grabs a microphone, and licks his lips. He turns on the microphone, bringing about a pleasant *ding*, and he chuckles to himself. The chuckle echoes in the habitat, and he looks around with wide eyes and a whimsical smile.

"Oh, wow, that's cool," says Crow, his voice overlapping with the speakers. "I've always wanted to mess with intercoms when I was a kid. Testing... Testing! Testing, one-two-three! Testing, one-two-three!"

*****

Raven skids to a stop in a pathway, and she looks side to side while pirates shout in the distance with Crow's voice echoing in the halls. When the pirates get close, she ducks into a dimly lit arcade room. Inside is a huddled group of people. Raven closes and locks the door and motions everyone to stay quiet. Seconds later, the pirates pass. One of them tries opening the door, but an error alarm dings, and the pirate leaves, telling the others the door is locked.

*****

Elsewhere in the habitat, Ibis shoves Sparrow into a mop closet and locks the door. Pirates hurry by, shouting at screaming civilians. Ibis presses his ear against the door while Sparrow grabs a broom as a weapon.

"What is it? What's going on?" asks Sparrow.

"Pirates. Lots and lots of pirates," says Ibis.

"Crap. And my bodyguard isn't here, either. I'm docking her pay if I don't see her soon."

Ibis nods. "Yeah, hopefully she shows up."

*****

Robin is hiding underneath a party table, eyes wet, body trembling, and her teeth sinking into her hand to stifle her whimpers, watching as multiple pirates shove civilians into rooms. But three people are making a commotion as the pirates drag them in front of Bellona's statue. She can't see much, but she hears plenty. And all this happening while the intercom blares various testing numbers and phrases.

"The quick brown fox jumps over the lazy dog; the lazy dog bites the quick brown fox; the quick brown fox dies and dies and dies, and cow jumped over the moon while cat ran with the spoon!" says Crow over the intercom. *"Man, this is cool. I love this. I'm gonna get an intercom for my ship when I'm done with this place!"*

Meanwhile, the three people are lined up and the pirates aim their weapons at them. Robin can't break her eyes away from what she is seeing.

"What is the meaning of this? You can't treat me like this! We had a deal!" yells Dunlin.

"Where's my money! I was promised money for helping you!" says Chick.

"Please, what's going on? Can't we speak to Crow?" begs Mavis.

"Nothing personal. You three were just part of the job," says Oro.

"Please no!" sobs Mavis.

"Wait, no!" cries Dunlin.

"Ah shit," sighs Chick.

Multiple gunshots of various speeds and volume ring out, and Robin bites down on her hand under the table while Dunlin, Chick, and Mavis drop dead.

The pirates put an extra round in each of their heads and then walk away. This leaves Robin staring at the corpses, shivering, and suffocating from keeping her sobs quiet.

"Okay, time to get serious! My name is Crow Magnolia, and I am your new captain!" says Crow over the intercom.

*****

Blackbird is quickly putting on the dead officer's vest and equipment, occasionally peeking over his shoulder..

"Now, I know you guys are scared, and you have every right to be. It is not often pirates attack a habitat. And it is not often all the security drop dead from poison!"

Blackbird checks the guard's pistol. "So much for relaxation."

"But this event will be quick. And if everyone behaves, nobody else will get hurt."

*****

In the vault room, Nightingale is wearing her purple-tinted sunglasses and watching Talon intently. The other pirates are splitting their attention between the hallway and the intercom.

"But I'm only going to say this once, if anyone gets in our way, you will die," says Crow.

Nightingale smirks.

"Okay, that's it! Now, if everyone will please go to the nearest residence or business so we can lock you up, that would be great! We don't want anyone else getting hurt after all!"

*****

Crow turns off the intercom and reclines in his seat, with his feet back on the desk and his stress ball rolling in his hand.

"That was fun," says Crow. He looks at the bridge full of pirates being lazy and calmly chatting to themselves, and he frowns. "Now, this ain't gonna work. I don't need all of you here, so half of you go and help round up the loose peeps. The rest of you, stay here and watch the monitors."

Half of his pirate group leaves, and the rest scramble to take seats. Crow sighs and squeezes his stress ball in steady pulses. Now comes the waiting game, and with it, the lingering cloud of dread. He knows it will only be a matter of time before the military comes in, or before someone tries something stupid. But civilians will be easy to handle. It is the military he is worried about. He would much rather be done and out with their reward before they show up.

That said, on an optimistic note, getting their money shouldn't be too hard, since all the security is dead, and the vault is not too complicated, just tedious. Since he didn't see Jay, he can only assume he's held up somewhere.

So, overall, they are off to a good start, and if their luck holds, they won't have to worry about dealing with people interfering with their operation. This might be a good payday for everyone, and for that, he tries to put himself at ease.

Captured

"Fan out and find the others! Stuff them in whatever room you can!" orders Oro.

Robin keeps her hand over her mouth and watches the boots spread around. When she no longer sees the boots, she listens for any movement. Their steps and voices quickly fade, and when she doesn't hear anybody, she cautiously lifts the tablecloth and peeks around.

She doesn't see anybody, but she does see the torn-up corpses of Dunlin, Mavis and Chick. So she quickly crawls out and scurries across the floor on her hands and knees, avoiding the trash and spilled food and drinks. When she reaches a door, she presses herself against the wall and slowly stands up. Then she gets in front of the sensor and the door opens with a soft whir.

Robin runs down the hallway, breathing heavily and focused on the elevator at the far end. She skids to a stop in front of the elevator and rapidly hits the button while looking over her shoulder.

The hallway door slides open, and three pirates enter. They briefly pause when they see Robin by the elevator, and she hits the button faster. The pirates yell at her and race down the hallway. The elevator dings and slides open.

Robin slips inside and hits the emergency close button right before the pirates reach her, and then hits the button for her hotel room's floor while the pirates bang on the elevator.

When the elevator reaches her floor, she carefully peeks out, sees no one, and starts running. Her steps echo in the hallway, and after she rounds the bend, three more pirates come around another corner, and immediately give chase to Robin. She stumbles as she changes directions and runs without any idea where she is going.

"Hey, stop!" yells a pirate.

Robin keeps running, and she looks over her shoulder and screams when she realizes that the pirates are gaining on her. She reaches a stairwell, but is tackled.

She and the pirate fall to the floor, and she grips the door frame, screaming for help while the pirates pull on her. Her fingers lose their grip, and she is dragged across the floor, pulled to her feet, and slammed against the wall with three guns aimed at her.

"W-Wait-wait! Don't hurt me-don't hurt me! I-I'm nobody special!" says Robin.

"The way you dress says otherwise," says the lead pirate. "Are you a supervisor? Do you work in *The City of Clouds* administration at any capacity?"

"No! N-No! I-I work for Arx Corporation!" stammers Robin.

"As a supervisor?"

"No! I'm a customer service representative!"

"So, you're one of those people who put us on hold for thirty minutes just to up-sell us stuff instead of fixing our problems?" says the second pirate.

"That's company policy! It's not my fault they're like that!"

Two of the pirates look at the third one, and he nods.

"She's right. My mom and I used to work customer service. Same thing she's telling us," says the third pirate.

"Sure, whatever, fine. But why are you out here, lady?" says the lead pirate.

"I-I was just going back to my hotel," stammers Robin. "It's just down there! Room 324!"

The three pirates close in on Robin, and she whimpers and holds her hands up protectively.

"Oh no. No. No-no-no- Don't do anything to me, please!" cries Robin.

The lead pirate grabs Robin's arm, and she shrieks and tries to pry the hand off while the pirate drags her down the hall. Every step is a struggle, and the other two keep an eye on the area as they walk down the hallway.

When they reach Robin's hotel room, the lead pirate shoves Robin to the door and aims his rifle at her.

"Room 324, right?" says the pirate.

"Y-Yes! Yes!" sobs Robin.

"Open it."

Robin's hands tremble as she fumbles with her key. When the door is opened, the pirate pushes her in, and the others enter with their weapons raised.

"Sit over there," orders the lead pirate, pointing at the chair in front of the window.

Robin's legs lose all strength when she sits down, and the pirates search her room, opening the drawers, cabinets, and doors. They take the cutlery away and close the door, leaving Robin alone in her room.

Then she hears something break and spark outside. She looks at her door and pales when warning lights swirl above it.

"Hey!" Robin runs to the door and tries to open it, but it doesn't work. She bangs on the door. "Hey! What did you do!?"

A small screen next to her beeps, and Robin turns it on, showing the three pirates outside.

"We broke your door so you can't get out. We don't need you wandering around during our operation. Stay there, behave, and you won't have anything to worry about from us," says the lead pirate.

The three pirates leave after that. Robin goes to her seat and stares at Bellona's eye with her arms across her chest and her tear-soaked face twisted from the fear eating her.

"Why me?"

*****

Back on the bridge, Crow is flipping through the instruction's manual while squeezing his stress ball. It takes him a little bit of time, but after finding what he needs, he types on one of the computers, and it brings up a live camera feed of Jay Azure's suite. Crow smiles and adjusts the settings on the microphone.

"*Hola!* Hello! How goes it, Captain Jay Azure! Congratulations on winning your election!" says Crow.

Jay and his security detail look around. Then Jay walks to one of the cameras and stares at it with a forced smile.

"Why thank you, kind pirate. Did you enjoy the snacks and drinks?" says Jay.

"I didn't have any. I ate before I got here," says Crow.

"Shame. You're missing out. My chef is a good cook," says Jay.

"I wish I knew that sooner, because I just had her executed."

"I'm going to take a wild guess and say she's the one that poisoned the habitat security, and you got rid of her to tie up loose ends."

"You guessed correctly."

"Eh, good riddance to her then. Now, what do you want?"

"The money in your vault. All that sweet, sweet cash and gold coins, silver bars, precious nuggets, all of it. You can make this easy for all of us and tell me the combination, or you can be difficult and let people suffer."

"I think I'll let you suffer by dealing with my vault. There's no other vault like mine, guaranteed! I made sure of it."

"You're one of those cocky bastards, eh? Well, we just might pay you a visit to teach you some manners when we're done with your vault."

"I'm not going anywhere, so take your time and see me when you're ready."

Then the feed disconnects, and Crow's smile shifts to a small frown. He gives his stress ball a few more squeezes before one of the pirates manning a monitor calls him over. Crow approaches his workspace and looks at the screen.

"What's going on?" asks Crow.

"There's still a security guard on the loose. See?" says the pirate, pointing at the screen.

Crow stares at it, and scoffs in disbelief.

"Wow, it's a small galaxy after all," says Crow. "I never knew that guy's name, but I know faces. And that face..."

(((((O)))))

Crow was walking down the street of a shanty town, thick-rimmed glasses on, hair

65

dyed white, and wearing flashy clothes with crows drawn on his white sneakers. He has his arms around Nightingale's hip.

And then a door to a movie store suddenly opened and hit Crow in the face, and Blackbird stepped out wearing headphones and his hooded jacket.

"OH FUCK!" yelled Crow, holding his face.

Blackbird stopped and looked at Crow with wide eyes. Worried, Nightingale tenderly rubbed Crow's shoulder.

"Oh my gosh, are you okay?" said Nightingale. Then she glared at Blackbird. "What's wrong with you? Don't you know how to look!?"

"Oh man, I'm sorry," said Blackbird as he lowered his headphones. "I didn't see you there! The way the door is positioned and–"

Crow sniffed blood and waved dismissively. "Nah, it's all good. I've been hit by worse, and today's your lucky day. I'm a little too busy to beat you to death."

Crow laughed, Blackbird laughed, albeit nervously. While the two laugh, Crow looked at Nightingale.

"C'mon, babe, we've got more important things to worry about than this peeled potato," says Crow.

Nightingale and Crow push past Blackbird, and Blackbird looked at them nervously.

"So... we're cool?" said Blackbird.

"Yeah, we're cool, bro. Mistakes happen," said Crow.

"Alright, take it easy."

"You, too."

Blackbird quickly walked away, and Crow and Nightingale went inside to the store's office, killed five people, took money owed plus extra, and then set the place on fire.

(((((O)))))

Crow nodded with a smile, eyes looking at the light.

"After that, me and Nightingale went on our ship, jumped the system, and then we had sex for five hours. It was alright," says Crow.

Some of the pirates nod and murmur how impressed or amused they are, and others keep to themselves.

"Lucky," says one of the pirates.

"Yes, I am. And bring up information on that guard. I want to know who he is," says Crow. He goes back to the command desk and turns on the intercom. "Attention, will the lone security guard somehow still alive *please* find a pirate group to surrender themselves to so they can detain you humanely?"

*****

Bartholomew Blackbird stays against the wall as he travels down the hallway. He briefly stops to listen to the broadcast message, and then he looks at a camera hanging from the ceiling, pointed right at him. He shakes his head and keeps walking.

"No can do, pirate," says Blackbird.

"Oh, are we playing that game?" says Crow over the intercom.

Blackbird rounds a corner and sees another camera aimed at him. He keeps walking anyway.

"You got a lot of balls walking around like that out in the open with a pistol and baton, while my pirates have a lot more guns, ammo, and armor than you."

"Yeah, this is a bad idea, I'll admit that, but duty calls," says Blackbird.

"Come on, man. Don't be difficult."

Blackbird opens a door, peeks out, then does a quick sweep with his weapon and carefully goes down the hallway.

"Oh, what do we have here? An impostor? Your vest number does not match your face," says Crow.

Blackbird ignores him.

"Alright, I can also see that you're going to be a problem, so here's the deal. There's a pretty girl that my pirates just stuffed in Room 324. If you do not surrender, Room 324 will have the air sucked out and she will suffocate. You have ten minutes."

The intercom clicks off, and Bartholomew swears and runs down the hallway.

*****

On the bridge, Crow is watching Blackbird run down the hallway. The other camera feed has the pirates that apprehended Robin walking down the hallway near her hotel room, and Crow activates his communicator. The camera shows their audio boxes being projected in front of them.

"Stay close to Room 324. Our impostor is on the way," says Crow.

"Roger that."

The pirates go back to Room 324, and Crow returns to squeezing the stress ball. Then he looks at another camera feed. This one is focused on Nightingale's team working on the vault. Progress is slow, but he is still not too worried. Plenty has gone right so far, and what harm can one loose impostor guard do, anyway?

Engage

Robin stands on her chair, pushing against the vent with a broom. The vent breaks free after some struggle, and Robin goes to the kitchen, grabs a garbage bag, and proceeds to turn it into a poncho.

After that, she returns to the chair, grabs the vent, and tries pulling herself up. She grunts, grits her teeth, and flexes her muscles as she lifts herself up. Then her grip slips, she falls, and breaks the chair upon landing. The momentum sends her rolling on the floor and getting a face full of carpet.

"Ow..." groans Robin.

After taking a moment to recuperate, Robin sits on her knees and rubs her head. She looks at the broken chair, and then at the bed. She goes to the bed and checks it, finding that it isn't bolted down. So, she grabs the bed's headrest, and gives it a pull.

The bed might as well have weighed a ton as it dragged against the carpet, tearing the fiber. Robin growls, re-positions herself, and gives the bed another tug. The bed shifts again, and Robin's legs and arms strain as she painstakingly drags it across the floor.

When she finally gets the bed where she wants it, there is a trail of torn carpet, and she is panting and sweating. She takes a few deep breaths, rubs her hands, and then goes onto the bed and jumps to the vent again.

She latches to the vent's opening and restarts her struggle. Her arms and abdomen burn, her legs kick, and she grinds her teeth and mutters insults to herself as she slowly and painfully pulls herself up. When she gets far enough up, she braces her hands against the vent's interior and cries as she pulls herself in.

Robin shifts and wiggles with every inch, and the garbage bag poncho tears as it is rubbed between her clothing and the metal plates. In a painful amount of time, Robin's torso gets far enough in, and soon her dangling hips join her in the vent, quickly followed by her legs.

The vent is dim with small lights, and Robin is panting heavily. Her limbs bump into the vent as she rubs her sweaty hair, and she takes a deep breath and looks down the passage.

"Okay... Straight... And... where... to go now?" wonders Robin. Her eyes shift, going from straight down the passage to looking at a corner. "Where? Where? Where?"

Robin takes another breath, shakes her head, and crawls forward.

"Forget it. I'm going straight. Then I'm going to hide in another room. I will not be suffocated by a bunch of pirates!"

*****

Out in the hallway, the pirates stare at the ceiling while Robin's muffled voice travels from a vent grate. They look at each other, one shrugs, and then they follow her voice.

*****

Blackbird opens a door and peeks down the stairway with his pistol drawn. He doesn't see or hear anyone, so he cautiously enters while the door clicks shut. He stays near the wall and walks down the steps, keeping his sights leveled. When he reaches the bottom, he peeks out the door window.

Again, nothing.

He carefully slips out. The door automatically shuts behind him, and he goes down the hallway, keeping his steps quiet as he passes a long TV screen with alternating advertisements. He hears some rattling in the vents. He looks up and follows the noise with his eyes, but when it fades, he takes a breath and goes around the corner.

Then he freezes.

Not too far from him are three pirates with rifles.

They stare at him. He stares at them.

Then both sides snap their weapons up.

"FREEZE!" barks Blackbird.

"Put your weapon down!" yells a pirate.

"No, you put your weapons down, now!"

"Put down your weapon!" shouts a pirate.

"Fuck you! Drop yours!" orders Blackbird.

"Put it down now!" yells another pirate.

"Don't make me shoot!" says Blackbird.

"DROP IT NOW!" screams a pirate.

Blackbird fires off a round, striking a pirate in the head. The other two swear and shoot back while Blackbird dives around the corner. Bullets fly and ricochet off the walls and floor, blowing out some lights and breaking the pots holding plants.

Blackbird shoots blindly around the corner until his magazine is empty. After he removes it, he fumbles with his new magazine.

When he slips it in, a pirate rounds the corner and attempts to bash his head with the rifle. He ducks, narrowly avoiding it, and screams as he slams the pirate into the wall across from him.

He follows up with a punch, quickly flips his pistol, and whacks it against the other pirate's rifle as they fire. The bullets bounce off the floor.

Blackbird is put in a choke hold, causing him to drop his pistol. He kicks the first pirate away, elbows his choker, and follows with a reverse headbutts until his grip loosens enough for him to swing him off.

The pirate rolls to the floor, and the one Blackbird kicked away draws his pistol.

Blackbird rushes him, and the two wrestle over the weapon, grunting and cursing and going in circles. When they are close enough to the second pirate, Blackbird kicks him in the face, and then he snaps the pistol down and shoots his target in the foot.

The pirate howls, and Blackbird twists the pistol and empties the magazine into the pirate's vest. Blood splashes out on Blackbird and the wall, and the pirate crumbles.

The remaining pirate roars and rams Blackbird into the wall, breaking the TV screen, now displaying an advertisement for a dentist. Sparks fly, skin burns from the sparks, and the pirate draws a knife.

Blackbird catches the attack when they bring the blade down, and he kicks out the pirate's footing and swings him into the TV, breaking more of the screen.

The pirate delivers swift, hard punches to Blackbird's sides and shoves him back. Blackbird quickly regains himself and draws his baton, and the pirate roars again and rushes him.

The pirate swipes, Blackbird dodges, then whacks the pirate's wrist and follows up with a strike to the head that knocks him to the ground, completely limp. After that is said and done, Blackbird is panting heavily. He swallows and looks at the two pirates. Then he goes around the corner and looks at his first kill. His hands tremble, his breathing is ragged, and he wipes his face with a bloody hand.

"Shit... Shit..." says Blackbird quietly.

Then the intercom clicks on.

"Officer Impostor, you just made a huge mistake. Consider yourself hunted," says Crow. *"And that nice looking piece of ass in Room 324? Yeah, she's dead, too."*

An emergency light suddenly turns on down the hall. Blackbird's eyes widen, and he runs towards Robin's room. He reaches it in a matter of seconds. The light is above Room 324, with a projector warning of a fire and alerting everyone that the air is being sucked out and warning of decompression if the door is opened during the process. He also sees that the door has been damaged.

"Robin!" calls Blackbird. He bangs on the door. "Robin! Shit."

Blackbird quickly searches the door and the surrounding area. He finds a panel next to the door with an *"Emergency Only"* printed on it. He opens it and sees a swipe pad with the security symbol above it,

He swipes his badge, and a pulley with yellow and black bands is revealed. He tugs on the pulley, and there is a loud pop, a hiss, and a sudden rush of air surging into the room. An alarm rings and foam sprays out from the ceiling, covering Blackbird, the hallway, and Room 324 in the mess.

Blackbird coughs and sputters as the white foam covers him, and yet he still rushes in, looking like a foam monster.

"Robin!" calls Blackbird.

He looks around the apartment, heart racing, and breathing ragged from panic. Then his wide eyes lock on the bed underneath the broken vent. He rushes to the setup, brushes the foam off himself enough to draw a flashlight, and he shines his light at the vent opening.

"Robin! Are you up there!" calls Blackbird.

Silence.

Blackbird calls for Robin again, but when he does not get a response, he looks around for something he can use to climb. While looks around, he stops, turns to the bathroom, and after a couple of seconds, he cautiously approaches it. He leans against the door and knocks.

"Robin? Are you in there?" says Blackbird.

He waits for a few seconds before opening the door with his pistol raised. The bathroom is empty and ransacked. Blackbird sighs, lowers his pistol, turns, and then swears and dives into the bathroom.

The last pirate, with a bleeding gash on his head, sprays the area with his rifle, leaving dents in the wall, piercing the door, and shattering the mirror. Blackbird presses himself against the wall and aims his pistol at the doorway.

When the pirate comes into view, Blackbird shoots him in the chest with the remaining rounds in his magazine. The vest holds, but the pirate stumbles back. Blackbird ejects the spent magazine and realizing that his other magazines are covered in foam, he charges the pirate with a vicious roar.

Their bodies clash, and they crash into the love seat and fall to the floor. They roll around, dealing punches and awkward kicks that quickly leave them bloodied and bruised.

During the scuffle, the pirate draws a knife and attempts to stab Blackbird. He catches it and forces the pirate to the side, putting them in a roll that leaves Blackbird on top. Blackbird disarms the pirate but is kicked off.

They scramble to their feet. The pirate snatches his knife, Blackbird draws his baton, and the pirate swings his blade wildly, forcing Blackbird back.

After a few more swipes, the pirate lunges, and Blackbird leaps out of the way. The knife stabs the TV, and Blackbird whacks the pirate with his baton.

The pirate retaliates with a slash to Blackbird's face that almost cuts him open, but he steps back just in time and slips on a broken chair piece that causes him to crash onto his back, dropping his baton.

The pirate kicks the baton away. Blackbird kicks out his footing and follows up with a leg swipe that brings the pirate down hard.

While the pirate gets back up, Blackbird takes a broken chair leg, whacks the knife out of the pirate's hand, and then plunges its jagged tip into his throat, ripping apart the flesh and arteries and poking out at an angle.

The pirate stumbles back, gurgling blood with more crimson pouring and spraying through the hole out of his throat. Then he falls backwards, hits his head on the bed frame, and crumbles in a twisted mess on the ground.

Blackbird stares at the corpse. Looking at the blood covering the foam all over him, he sighs heavily and collects the pirate's rifle, ammo, and knife. They also have the same model pistol, so he also takes that ammo. Once he is all set, Blackbird wipes the foam off himself and exits the room.

"So much for vacation," grumbles Blackbird.

In the Vents

Robin whimpers and crawls fast through the vent as gunshots echo not too far from her. Her makeshift poncho is now tattered plastic strips, and thin amount of dust clings to her clothes, giving her faint gray streaks.

She comes to a stop at crossroads. Both directions look the same, and she bites her lip, her eyes darting left and right and her thoughts a blur as she struggles to decide which direction to go. The shooting isn't helping her situation either. The only upside is that the gunfire is slowing down. And even then, that might not be an entirely good thing for her.

"Okay, where to next?" mutters Robin. She holds up her finger and... "Hana, man, mona, mike; Barcelona, bona, strike; hare, ware, frown, vanac; Harrico, warico, we wo, wac!"

Robin's finger stops left. So, she goes left.

Her knees scuff against the vent's floor as she crawls. When she reaches a vent grate, she peeks down and sees more pirates patrolling. She freezes and watches them, and one of the pirates lights a cigarette.

"This is dumb. There's no way we can control this whole habitat," says a pirate.

"We don't have to. We control just enough to get the money and get out. No more, no less," says another pirate.

"And what about Jay Azure?" says the third pirate.

"We'll see what Crow says. I'm indifferent if he lives or dies. I just want his money," says the first pirate.

Then the intercom dings.

"Attention citizens of The City of Clouds, this is your captain speaking," says

Crow. *"It has come to my attention that there is a troublemaker on the loose, pretending to be a security guard. He's already killed three pirates, which means he has escalated things. Now, I'm not under the delusion that everyone is locked tight on this habitat, so I'm going to make myself clear. If anyone helps Officer Impostor, they will be killed along with him. Okay, that's it!"*

The intercom clicks off, and one of the pirates curses while the group checks their weapons.

"Come on, let's find that prick," says the first pirate.

The group hurries away, and Robin takes a deep breath and continues traveling through the vent, keeping her movements slow. She tries to keep her breathing steady, and her ears are on alert as she hears pirates rush by her, giving orders.

Soon Robin comes to another crossroads and recites the rhyme again. This time, she goes right and takes a slide down a sudden, steep incline. She shrieks and presses her hands against the wall, and her feet spread out just enough to stop her slide. Now her heart is racing, and her breathing is shaky.

"Did you hear that?" asks a pirate nearby.

"The shrieking?" asks another.

"Yeah. Where did it come from?"

"Sounds like the vents."

Then there is a thump against the vent near Robin.

"Hello? Anybody in there?" asks the first pirate.

"You think it's that one guy?" asks the second pirate.

"If it is, then they have a really girly scream." The thumping returns. "Hey! Anybody up there!"

Robin bites her lip, squeezes her eyes shut, and makes a deep, long inhale, followed by an exhale. Her eyes open, and she releases her grip.

She slides down the vent and shields her head with her arms when she lands at the vent's plateau. She bounces a bit, but quickly recovers and crawls as fast as she can, not caring about the ruckus of her shaking the vent.

"I knew it! There's someone's in the vent!" shouts a pirate.

"It's gotta be Officer Impostor!" yells another.

"BLAST HIM!" orders a third pirate.

Gunfire rings out, and bullet holes appear in the vent, narrowly missing Robin. Light pours in through the holes, and Robin shrieks and crawls faster, heart racing and vision getting hazy from tears. She takes a turn and comes across a vent grate with a lever on the inside. She pulls the lever, and the grate slides open, revealing an elevator shaft with cables dangling.

Robin pokes her head out and sees the large, reinforced springs at the shaft's bottom. She tilts her head up and sees the lights of an elevator, all the way at the cloud's final floor, and tiny lights mark a ladder near her.

Robin's hands tremble as she grabs the ladder. She slowly pulls herself out and gasps from the drop of leaving the elevator. Her other hand and feet catch the ladder, and she presses herself against it, quivering and whimpering.

After a moment of being stationary, Robin looks up, swallows, and reaches up to the next ladder rung. She pulls herself up, and repeats. Soon, she is climbing at a steady pace passing vents as she goes. But after a minute of climbing, there is a beep, and lights start flashing.

Robin looks up, and her eyes bulge. The lights are coming from the elevator. She sees the nearest vent is a few feet down, and its grate has a lever.

The elevator whirs and the cables begin shifting. Robin quickly climbs down and the elevator descends.

Robin pulls the lever. The vent grate slides open, and she reaches out. The elevator is rapidly getting closer.

She grabs an interior handle and pulls herself inside. The air is getting pushed down as the elevator drops, and Robin's legs are tucked in, right as the elevator passes her and grinds to a stop.

Robin curls up in the vent and bites her hand as she rocks back and forth. The elevator dings, and footsteps sound off below her.

"Alright, where is he?" asks a pirate.

"Crow is saying he's in this pod," says another.

"Alright, block off all the exits and keep your ears open. One of the teams said they heard somebody in the vents."

"Was it Officer Impostor?"

"Nah. Unless he's got a lot of estrogen."

"Hey, are you two done chit-chatting? We got a pod to secure!" says a third pirate.

"Yeah, we're coming... Let's go."

The pirates walk away, and Robin stays still. Waiting. Listening.

Nothing happens after a minute, and the elevator is still blocking her way, so she goes forward, making sure to travel slow, especially when passing over a vent grate. She sees a pair of pirates walking cautiously around, so she waits until they are out of sight before inching forward. She keeps going until she hears a scuffle. There are grunts, shouts, bangs, and crashes, and Robin's heart races as she peeks through the nearest vent grate.

She sees Blackbird has already knocked out one of the pirates and is fighting the other two with his baton. They have had their rifles disarmed, and his swings are swift and brutal. Each strike is met with a loud crack and cry.

After a few more seconds of fighting, one pirate is left on the ground with his head bleeding, and the other barely draws their knife before they are disarmed. Then, Blackbird strikes the back of their leg and follows up with a hard whack to their head that leaves them limp on the ground.

Robin quietly watches Blackbird panting and rummaging through the bodies, and then a camera turns to him.

"Officer Impostor, you really can't be doing this," says Crow.

"Why not? You're the one that ruined my vacation, and a date night," says Blackbird.

"Because if you keep this up, I will suck the air out of another room. Maybe a bigger one with more people in it?"

"Like what you did to that poor girl in Room 324?"

"She didn't have to die. But if you don't surrender, then more people will die, and that will be blood on your hands."

"I'm not surrendering to you."

Crow chuckles. *"Alright then. Try to hold back the tears when I take more lives."*

The intercom clicks off, and Blackbird checks his pistol.

"Psst!" calls Robin.

Blackbird jumps and looks around with his pistol at the ready.

"Blackbird. Up here," whispers Robin.

Blackbird looks up. "Robin? You are in the vents! Are you okay?"

"Better than expected. The vents being cleaner than I thought helps."

"Yeah... Priorities, I guess."

"We need to get out of this cloud. I think if we go through the vents, we can escape."

"Good idea. Meet me in the broom closet over there." Blackbird points in the direction he wants Robin to go. "Crow has control of the cameras, and there's definitely more pirates coming, so we have to make it quick."

Robin nods. "Okay, I'll meet you over there."

Blackbird runs off, and Robin crawls towards the broom closet. After she reaches the ventilation above the room, she removes the vent grate. Blackbird closes and jams the closet door, and then he brings a ladder over.

Seconds later, there is a banging on the door, and Blackbird leaps up, grabs the vent, and easily pulls himself in, with only a short grunt. This leaves Robin's face hot and mind flustered.

"Cover the vent, and let's get out of here," says Blackbird.

Robin returns the vent grate to its original position and follows Blackbird down the tunnel. His bigger frame and weapons press against the walls, making consistent scrapes, and they can hear the door to the broom closet shot and forced open.

Blackbird crawls faster and Robin follows him. He makes a snap decision of turning left, so Robin follows, and when their bodies pass the corner entirely, they stop moving and Blackbird holds up his finger.

"Stay quiet," whispers Blackbird.

Robin nods and inches closer to Blackbird while coiling her body as much as she can. A few seconds later, the vent grate opens and a circle of light shines on the vent and goes side to side.

"Any signs of him?" asks a pirate.

"Nope," says the pirate in the vent. "And these vents are clean, so there's no dust or anything to use. It's very impressive how clean this vent is, to be honest. We really need to do that for our ship."

"Well, the captain's already wanting an intercom, so maybe we can get one of them fancy vent cleaning robot things too while he's in a good mood."

"Maybe. But we'll have to alert the others to keep an eye on the vents. No telling where Officer Impostor will pop up now."

The light disappears, the vent closes, and Robin and Blackbird remain still for a few moments before Robin takes a deep, nervous breath, and asks, "So... Now what?"

"Now, we go to the engine room and take control of the air supply," says Blackbird.

Bickering Couple

Ibis opens the broom closet and pokes his head out to scan the area. With the coas clear, he waves Sparrow forward.

"Let's go," says Ibis.

"Where?" asks Sparrow.

"To a lifeboat."

"Wait, so you're going to abandon all these poor people to these pirates? How cruel. How heartless! How... **soulless.**"

Ibis frowns at Sparrow, and Sparrow is clenching his heart, while standing under a dim light with his head bowed and shadows covering much of his face.

"Feel better?" asks Ibis.

"No." Sparrow snaps up. "We still have to save these people from the pirates."

"Officer Impostor can handle it."

"What about the girl?"

"What girl?"

"Chickadee."

"Chickadee?"

"The girl with poor fashion sense."

"That's Robin."

"Chickadee."

"Fine. What about *Chickadee*?"

"Don't you want to save her?"

Ibis stares at Sparrow, and the journalist slides to him and puts his hand on his arm.

"I've seen you two talking. There's got to be a click going on, so if you don't want to stay to help them, stay to help her," says Sparrow.

Ibis sighs and looks down. "Fine… But I have no idea where to start."

"You don't have to look anywhere," says Sparrow. "All we have to do is go to the communications room, send out an S-O-S, and then the military comes by, and we get to be heroes!"

"Okay, but how do we get to the communications room?" says Ibis.

Sparrow holds up his finger, takes a deep breath, and says, "Step one, we need a map. Step two, we read the map to find the communications room. Step three, we go to the communications room. Step four, we send out the signal. Step five, we wait. Step six, you kiss Chickadee."

"I'm not kissing her."

"Why not?"

"Because… reasons."

Sparrow grins. "Is that a dark secret I sense? That's wonderful! You'll have to tell me the details when this is over!"

"How about I tell you never."

Before Sparrow can reply to this, Ibis leaves, and Sparrow leans out of the closet and watches him go.

"Ibis?" says Sparrow.

Ibis quickly rounds the corner.

"Ibis! … Dang it," grumbles Sparrow.

Ibis walks down the hallway with brisk steps while Sparrow tails him. Soon they enter an expansive area with concrete, raised beds filled with soil and plants, and above them are UV lights and mist machines. Furniture is arranged in ways for optimal socializing, and pillars of digital screens with various advertisements are spaced evenly, while warning messages scroll across digital bands near the ceiling. There are also large, curved windows that show Bellona's chaotic swirling bands.

Ibis scans the area for signs of trouble, or a map, and when he sees a map of the habitat on the wall, he approaches it. But right as he reaches it…

"IBIS!" shrieks Sparrow.

Ibis turns around and sees Sparrow being held hostage by a pirate that is pressing a pistol against his head. A group of four more pirates are with him. Two are aiming their weapons at Sparrow, and two are aiming at Ibis.

"Don't do anything stupid," says a pirate.

Ibis sighs and raises his hands and slowly goes to his knees.

Within a few short minutes, Ibis and Sparrow have their wrists bound and are taken to a break room with vending machines, a table, and a couch. A warning message is displayed on the TV, and arts and crafts supplies are on the counter with some homemade signs crafted to celebrate Jay Azure's victory.

"Alright, nobody do anything stupid, and nobody will get hurt, got it?" says a pirate.

Ibis and Sparrow nod, kneeling on the floor and glaring at them. The pirates leave and lock the door, and Ibis immediately begins wiggling and flexing his hands and wrists, and Sparrow shakes his head in disbelief.

"I can't believe this," says Sparrow.

"What?" says Ibis.

"I still don't know where my bodyguard is," says Sparrow. "She should be coming in, guns blazing and beating up bad guys. Like those action chicks in the movies."

Ibis stops fidgeting and looks over his shoulder at Sparrow. "You do realize movies are embellishments of reality, right?"

"Yeah, I know, but I hired a bodyguard, and so far, all I got out of her was her cake. Which wasn't even that good."

"She gave you cake?"

"Yeah. She donated it to me."

"Like, a whole cake or a slice?"

"A slice. It was strawberry."

"Frosting?"

"Also strawberry. But it was the nasty kind that always tastes stale."

Ibis resumes wiggling and working on the zip tie. "Where did you find her, anyway?"

"Dave's List. She specifically said any job, so I hired her to be a bodyguard," says Sparrow.

Ibis stops working his wrists and looks at Sparrow again with a small sneer. "Are you serious?"

Now Sparrow looks at him, visibly annoyed. "Yes. Why are you sounding like you're about to blow a gasket?"

"Because it's Dave's List! It sucks!"

"They have great prices!" says Sparrow defensively. "Did you know you could hire private investigators and hitmen on there? You just need to know the right words."

Ibis groans and cranes his head toward the ceiling. "Oh my God. How did you figure that out!?"

"ReadIt."

Ibis works harder on the zip ties and awkwardly stomps the floor. "Oh, fucking hell. Why would you look that up?"

"It was a rabbit hole! It all started when I researched myself to see if anyone recognized my benign contributions to society."

"Bullshit."

"It is not."

"Yes, it is! And you know what? I'm having you gagged for being stupid. Pirate!" calls Ibis.

The door opens and a pirate goes to Ibis.

"What do you want?" asks the pirate impatiently.

"Can you gag this man? He's an idiot," says Ibis.

The pirate looks at Sparrow, shrugs, and grabs a roll of tape from the counter and goes to Sparrow.

"Don't you dare! Do you know who I am!?" says Sparrow.

"Don't know. Don't care," says the pirate as he tapes Sparrow's mouth.

With the pirate distracted, Ibis breaks the zip tie binding him with one solid tug, grabs the pirate, and puts him in a choke hold while drawing his pistol. The pirate gags and tries prying him off, but Ibis's strength is too much for the pirate.

The pirate's struggle dwindles, his breathing becoming more labored and his gags weaker. Then the pirate goes limp. The whole time this happens, Ibis keeps his eyes and pistol on the door, and even after his target goes limp, Ibis keeps him in his grip.

"Hey, you okay in there? What's going on?" calls another pirate from outside.

The door opens, and Ibis puts a bullet in his head, making Sparrow release a muffled shriek. The pirate crumbles, and the others outside curse.

Ibis throws away his meat shield and moves off to the side. Sparrow flops to the floor and worm-crawls his way behind a couch, and Ibis goes by the open door and peeks out. Bullets fly, almost striking him. He pulls the corpse to him and closes and locks the door.

Bullets strike the door, and Ibis swiftly grabs the dead pirate's rifle and knife and puts on their vest. Ibis checks the rifle, and then the door is blown open. Ibis's ears ring and the destroyed door lays on the floor. The pirates rush in, and Ibis shoots one at close range through the sides.

His target drops dead, and Ibis rams his rifle stock against the face of the closest attacker, pivots, and shoots at the others. The shots are sloppy, but they do their job in forcing the other two pirates to back off.

Ibis quickly finishes off the pirate he struck and sprays the outside area again.

The remaining two pirates scramble for cover as the bullets rip apart furniture, shatter potted plants, and destroy pillars depicting digital advertisements.

"We need reinforcements! Section D-1! Now!" barks a pirate into his radio.

Ibis slides to cover behind a concrete raised bed and shoots blindly over it.

The pirates shoot back, chipping away at the concrete and spilling the soil. The plants are torn by the bullets, and Ibis runs to the nearest pirate, shooting as he goes.

When he is at his target, he rams his rifle stock against his head. The pirate crumbles, and Ibis is shot in the vest, knocking him off his feet.

The pirate he hit gets up on his hands and knees, and Ibis kicks him away. Then he shoots the other pirate while on his back. He keeps shooting until they crumble to the ground, twitching and bleeding profusely.

Ibis then goes to the pirate he kicked away, shoots him through the head, and pulls a grenade off his vest. When the stairwell door opens, he primes the grenade and throws it at the arriving group.

The group curses and scramble away, and an explosion destroys the door. As the smoke settles, Ibis gets on his knee with his rifle aimed at the doorway, panting heavily.

Pirates poke their heads out but are forced back when Ibis sprays their area. He backs up, and ducks behind another concrete, raised bed when the pirates shoot back. Then Sparrow slides next to Ibis.

"Hi!" says Sparrow, holding a knife in his bloody hand and a red band across his face.

"Shit!" yells Ibis, almost hitting Sparrow with his rifle. "Don't do that!"

More bullets fly, and Ibis shoots back.

"How did you get out, anyway?" says Ibis.

"The guy you choked out had a knife, so I took it and cut my way out. Were you planning on leaving me?"

More bullets fly from both sides.

"It crossed my mind, but I wasn't," says Ibis.

"At least you're honest," says Sparrow.

"You should try it some time. It feels good."

Sparrow balks, and the pirates rush out from the stairwell, shooting wildly in Ibis's direction. Ibis and Sparrow crouch lower. During the chaos, Ibis looks around and sees an illuminated sign pointing to the elevator.

"Get to the elevator. I'll cover you," says Ibis.

Sparrow nods, and Ibis slips a new magazine in and sprays the area, forcing the pirates into cover. Sparrow runs, and Ibis follows close behind.

"Don't look back! Just run!" orders Ibis.

Bullets destroy the environment around them, and Sparrow almost falls over when he rounds the corner. Ibis presses himself against the wall when he gets around the corner a couple seconds later, and he shoots again.

Sparrow reaches the elevator and hits the button until the door opens. Then he holds the door while waving at Ibis.

"Come on!" shouts Sparrow.

Ibis shoots off a few more rounds, and then runs to the elevator. Once he is in, Sparrow releases the door and hits the emergency close button. He presses the button for the engine room. The elevator hums and gears crank, and Ibis paces and checks his weapons while Sparrow slumps against the wall.

"That was nuts. I didn't know you could do that," says Sparrow.

"I was a child soldier on Alkhatib and after I left, I was an freelance photographer for the Oros Crime Wars, and an unofficial war photographer for the Aarde Conflict. I learned a few things during those times."

"How old are you again?"

"That's rude."

"Fine, be a prude. But just know that I'll be giving you Raven's money since you're a better bodyguard than she is."

Ibis smiles tiredly. "I'm okay with that."

*****

On the bridge, Crow is looking at the mess left by Ibis and Sparrow. His hand squeezes his stress ball tightly, and his jaw clenches while ragged breaths leave through his nose. He watches the terrible pair go into the elevator, and opens up the habitat manual, flips to where he needs to go, and quickly types in some commands. After he types in the commands, he brings up Oro on his communicator.

"Oro, we have more problems," says Crow.

*****

Inside the elevator, calming music plays, and Sparrow and Ibis shift in their spots. Both have adrenaline surging through them. Ibis is constantly checking his rifle and shifting from one foot to another, and Sparrow drums on his hand and walks in a circle.

Then the music stops, the elevator jerks to a halt, and all the warm lights are replaced with harsh yellow lights. A robotic voice then says, *"Elevator services have been suspended. If you are in an elevator at this time, assistance will be given. Thank you for choosing* The City of Clouds *and have a wonderful day."*

87

Ibis and Sparrow stare at the intercom in the corner, and Sparrow sighs heavily and taps his fingers hard on his hand.

"Wow, their customer service still sucks monkey balls," says Sparrow.

Ibis looks at the emergency exit on the ceiling. "Well, we can't stay here, so I hope you're ready to work your muscles."

Sparrow looks at the emergency exit and seethes. "Yeah, I kinda flunked gym class, so I'm not good with this whole 'muscles' thing. But I also don't want to die by pirates, so... You go first. If it's safe, you can pull me out. If not, I'll take my chances here. We both win!"

"Sure. Whatever." Ibis shoulders his rifle and rubs his hands together. "Okay... Let's do this."

Battle in the D-Cloud

It has been a while since escaping the pirates, and Robin is trailing Blackbird. Her plastic bag poncho is now strands hanging around her neck and the fabric on her knees is starting to tear. They take turns here and there as they traverse the vents, occasionally stopping to listen for trouble. But in one instance, after rounding a corner, Blackbird suddenly shouts, "Shit!"

He jumps, bangs his head on the vent ceiling, and curses again while scrambling back and hitting Robin. As this happens, Ibis reels back. He bumps into Sparrow, forcing him back.

"What's going on?" asks Robin.

"Get your butt out of my face!" says Sparrow.

"What the hell are you doing here?" says Blackbird.

"I'm trying to live. What are you doing here?"

"*I'm* trying to live."

Ibis looks at Blackbird's outfit and notices the security vest over his jacket.

"Wait a minute. You're Officer Impostor!" says Ibis.

"Considering that all the security guards are dead, I had no choice but to take matters into my own hands," says Blackbird.

"Ibis is that you?" says Robin.

Ibis and Robin lean over at the same time, and Robin smiles brightly and waves at him. Ibis returns the wave before looking at Blackbird, who is studying his outfit.

"Why are you dressed like that? Aren't you a photographer?" asks Blackbird.

"I am, and I wanted to leave, but Sparrow convinced me to stay to help the people," says Ibis.

"I did," says Sparrow proudly.

"That's nice, but if you two could back up so we could get to the elevator, that would be great."

"We just came from there. They locked the elevators," says Ibis.

"Dang it," huffs Blackbird. "So, where are you heading?"

"We're going to the communications room to get a signal out to the military. You?"

"Engine cloud. We're going to reclaim the air supply."

"Want to join us? We can use more hands," says Robin.

Blackbird looks at Robin critically, she shrugs, and Ibis thinks for a moment.

"Getting control of the air supply is actually a great idea, but we will only accompany you if we go to the communications room next," says Ibis.

Blackbird nods. "Sounds good. But if the elevator is jammed, then we need to either take the stairs or service elevator."

"But the elevators are jammed," says Sparrow.

"Service elevators are always active. It is a feature of all habitats by Federation law."

"Oh. Neat."

"Well, it's been fun chatting in here, but we really need to get moving," says Ibis.

Blackbird nods and looks over his shoulder.

"Go back to where we came from, Robin," says Blackbird.

Robin nods and backs up, and Blackbird waves Ibis and Sparrow forward.

*****

Back on the bridge, Crow is skimming through the ship's schematics while he rolls the stress ball in his fingers. He's found notes of repairs, renovations, paint jobs, plant installations, and so on. Crow also has a view of his next targeted room; in case the survivors try something. Suddenly, his communicator turns on, and an audio box is projected in front of him.

"*We heard many voices in the vents,*" says a pirate, the lines jerking up and

90

down with the vocals. *"They are going to the engine cloud to secure the air. Then it is on to the communications room."*

Crow squeezes his stress ball. "Send reinforcements to those areas. Kill everyone in that group."

"Yes sir."

The pirate hangs up, and Crow brings up Oro's audio box.

"Oro, assemble a group and head to the engine cloud," says Crow.

"Yes sir," says Oro.

Crow hangs up, and then selects Nightingale for his next call.

*****

In the vault room, Nightingale remains focused on the drill. Light reflects off her sunglasses and thin, curled sheets of metal fly out with the sparks. Every so often, the drill is pulled back to replace the dulled drill bit with a new one.

"Tell me you have good news, my love," says Crow over the communicator.

"We have four of the safety poles disconnected," says Nightingale. "There are six remaining. Once those are removed, we should be able to open it without a problem."

"Good. When you get it open, get the money on our ship immediately," says Crow.

Nightingale looks over her shoulder at the stack of duffle bags, and smirks. "Way ahead of you."

*****

Raven peeks out of the arcade, and after a moment of scanning the area, she motions the others hiding in it out. They quickly and quietly file out, and she grabs one of the arcade workers.

"Do you know where the escape boats are?" asks Raven.

The worker nods. "Just one boat can easily hold all of us."

"Do you know how to use it?"

"He doesn't, but I do," says another worker, his uniform showing him to be maintenance.

"Good. Take them to the boat and get out of here."

"It sounds like you aren't going with us."

"I'm not. I have a job to do. Good luck, all of you."

Then Raven hurries away from the group, and as she goes to the elevator, she sees a red band on its light, so she takes the stairs instead. She spends the next few minutes evading pirates and cameras, and when she reaches her room, she retrieves her duffle bag from under the bed, and quickly assembles a pistol, loads its four magazines with bullets, and then grabs a multitude of explosive bricks and a remote detonator. She puts them in a backpack and hurries out of her room.

*****

Robin peeks through a vent grate and listens for any noise and watches for movement. Nothing is there, so she opens the vent grate, grips the edge tight, and peeks out further. The area is still clear in all directions, so she adjusts herself and drops down.

Upon landing, she hops away and mutters elementary curses due to the painful shocks in her shins. Blackbird and Ibis land without trouble, but Sparrow stumbles and falls over after jumping down.

Robin leans against a pillar, standing on one foot to rub her shin, and Ibis and Blackbird look around.

They are in a lobby with a circular observation window, and strips of curved glass that give a view of Bellona. A digital band stretches across the length of the lobby, advising people to stay in their apartments, and pillars with digital screens are placed evenly around the area, as well as TVs showing warning messages.

The lobby is also decorated with raised beds of plants, simple but comfortable furniture, and a map of *The City of Clouds*. At one end is a doorway pointing towards maintenance, and the other end has a door for the D-E Pathway.

Sparrow and Ibis go to the map, and Blackbird looks around, stopping when he sees a camera looking at them. His hand tightens on his rifle, and he hurries towards the maintenance door.

"We have to move," says Blackbird.

Robin follows him, and Ibis and Sparrow run after him after a few more seconds of studying the map. When they are halfway to the maintenance door, it flashes red, as does the door to the D–E Pathway. A door slides open at a raised location, as well as a door marking the C–D Pathway. Then pirates pour out with their weapons raised.

"There they are!" shouts a pirate.

"Run!" says Blackbird.

The group runs, and bullets fly. They seek cover behind raised beds, or tip over tables to use as cover before returning fire. They drop some of the pirates, but the assailants keep advancing.

"Keep pushing! And watch the glass!" shouts a pirate.

More bullets fly, causing carnage all over the lobby, and Robin crawls on her hands and knees, whimpering as she makes her way to Blackbird, who is quick to pull her to cover.

"Stay down!" says Blackbird.

He shoots again and is forced down as a barrage of bullets shred an advertisement pillar behind him.

Ibis leans out and guns down a pirate before ducking back into the cover.

"Blackbird, we need to get out of here!" says Ibis.

"I know!" says Blackbird. He looks down the length of the lobby and sees a clear opening to the D–E Pathway. "I'm opening that door! Cover me!"

Ibis nods and shoots at the pirates. Blackbird races to the D–E Pathway door, ducking and weaving while bullets streak past him. He slides to the floor, tips a table over, and uses it as a shield as he opens the door's panel and activates its emergency lever. The D–E Pathway door slides open, and Blackbird waves the group in.

"Go! Go! Go! Hurry!" says Blackbird.

Robin runs and dives into the Pathway. Sparrow follows her lead. Next is Ibis, and while Ibis shoots at the pirates from his doorway cover, Blackbird slides in and locks the door shut. Its light flashes red, and the group continues running.

"Get to the other side!" says Blackbird.

The group runs faster down the Pathway, which is nearly identical to the lobby, only it is a tube instead of a circular area. As they run, Robin hears a *ding*. She looks behind and she sees that the light is green, and the pirates are pouring through the open door.

"The pirates are in!" yells Robin.

Blackbird turns and shoots, dropping a pirate, and the group goes into cover while bullets zip towards them, destroying everything in their path. Blackbird and Ibis return fire, but they can only do potshots or shoot blindly.

"Move up! Kill them all!" orders a pirate.

*****

On the bridge, the stress ball is flat in Crow's grip. His jaw is tight and his eyes dart between every member of the group of troublemakers resisting him, but he keeps going back to Robin, who he was sure suffocated in the apartment. And he's also certain he knows her from somewhere.

"She's supposed to be dead," says Crow. "But she's not dead... And I know I know her, so who the hell is she?"

Crow paces and scratches his head.

"I know I know her from somewhere. Think. Think. Think."

As Crow paces, the shootout continues to be displayed on the monitors with the pirates on the bridge watching intently.

*****

Faint gunshots echo in *The City of Clouds* as Raven races down the hallway. Her heart races, and she wipes sweat off her forehead with her sleeve. She keeps her pistol held tight, and ducks for cover behind a raised concrete bed of miniature trees when a door opens.

"Let's go! Hurry your asses! We're cutting through the Communications Cloud!" says Oro.

The footsteps pass, and Raven peeks up and sees Oro and half a dozen other pirates go into a stairwell. After the last of them pass and the stairwell door closes, she takes a deep breath, and continues moving away from the gunshots.

*****

Back in the observation tube, Robin stays low, and scurries from one area to the next, yelping and whimpering as the bullets rip apart everything. The whole time, Bellona's eye watches, its lightning surging along the swirling gaseous bands.

Concrete bits, furniture guts, broken glass litter the floor. Display pillars and bands shatter and flicker from the bullets destroying them. Ibis and Blackbird do what they can to keep the pirates back, while Sparrow and Robin make their way down the tube.

"I'm running low!" says Blackbird.

Ibis tosses him a magazine and ducks by a stairwell leading to the upper level of the tube while glaring at Sparrow and Robin.

"Run faster!" yells Ibis.

Sparrow makes a break for it, but Robin curls on the floor and clutches her head, eyes sealed shut and ears ringing from the shouting and gunfire. Somehow in the chaos, she hears a clatter near her, and she opens her eyes.

A grenade is in front of her face.

Robin screams in fright and chucks it away from her. It sails in the air, then detonates, cracking the curved window with its shrapnel. The cracks grow, the glass groans, and in a split-second, it shatters.

Glass shards, furniture, and pirates are yanked into space, and a rush of air pulls Robin and her group across the floor.

Robin flips and bounces across the floor, hits the railing and spins over it. She grips the railing painful determination and pulls herself against it. She grits her teeth while her lungs are shriveled, and her feet are yanked into the air.

Blackbird hits an advertisement pillar, shattering the digital display.

Ibis is slammed into a concrete bed that has all its dirt and plants flying off into space.

And Sparrow gets stuck on the railing.

Furniture tumbles into the void and more pirates are sucked into space. Then a metal slab slides down, covering the hole. More slabs slide down, covering the rest of the curved windows, and red warning lights swirl in the dark.

Robin drops against the railing, then her grip slips and she makes a croaky scream as she falls on her back the next floor down.

Her lungs burn, her head is swimming, and a throbbing pain radiates across her body. Bullets fly, people shout, and Robin turns on her hands and knees, coughing and gagging.

Ringing stabs her ears. Her vision is unsteady, and she falls over again, wheezing and staring at the swirling red lights.

Tracers zip above her head, striking the metal plates or breaking warning lights. Then a body flips over the railing with Blackbird. They land near Robin with their rifles skidding away, and both scramble up at the same time.

Robin watches as she tries catching her breath. Blackbird gets the upper hand on the pirate, wrestles the pistol away, and shoots them through the bottom of their jaw. Blood splashes on the wall and the pirate goes limp. There is no pause as Blackbird sweeps the area with the pistol, and then he grabs his rifle and runs to Robin.

"Are you okay?" asks Blackbird.

"I... I..." Robin looks around at the empty area littered with dead pirates and blood, and she looks at Blackbird with distant eyes. "No..."

Blackbird grabs Robin's arm and pulls her to her feet, and Ibis and Sparrow come down the stairs a moment later.

"There she is! Good throw, Chickadee!" says Sparrow.

"Please don't do that again," says Ibis.

Robin nods and leans against Blackbird for support, and he scowls at the other two.

"How about asking if she's alright?" says Blackbird.

"I'm sorry... Are you okay, Robin?" says Ibis.

"She's standing. She's fine," says Sparrow with a dismissive wave.

Ibis and Blackbird glare at him, and Robin holds Blackbird tight.

"Can we get out of here, please?" asks Robin.

Blackbird nods. "Follow me."

The group follows Blackbird to the door, which has been sealed and has an emergency sign projected over it. He opens the panel next to the door, swipes his badge, and pulls a lever. The door slides open, nearly blinding everyone with how bright the other side is. Blackbird and Ibis take the lead with their rifles raised as they sweep the lobby they were in prior, with Bellona's eye staring at them as they file into the wrecked area.

"WARNING: DECOMPRESSION IN D–E PATHWAY. EVACUATE CLOUD D AND CLOUD E IMMEDIATELY!"

Said message repeats over the speakers, and Blackbird lowers his weapon and looks at Robin and Sparrow.

"We're going to need to arm you two," says Blackbird.

*****

Crow stares at the aftermath with a deep scowl. His fingers tear into the stress ball. He leans over and types in a command on one of the computers and watches its monitor with a small smile. When his objective is complete, he types in another command, and his grin grows while faint, panicked screams fill the air. Some of the pirates look outside, and they pale and step back and look at Crow with absolute shock.

"Captain! Are you mad!?" says one of the pirates.

"I am," says Crow, still smiling.

*****

Back in the lobby, Bellona's light shines on, bathing everything in a red tint as Ibis and Blackbird are collecting weapons and ammo. They give Robin and Sparrow a rifle and the vests from dead security and spend the next minute giving quick instructions on the safety, trigger, and sights, advising them on basic handling. During this quick lesson, Sparrow tests his rifle's weight and sights under Ibis's supervision, and Robin pales and trembles with the weapon in her hand.

"I don't know if I can do this. I mean, I don't know if I can kill anybody. I've never done anything with a weapon. I haven't even played laser tag or paintball!" says Robin frantically.

"Girl, you just launched a bunch of pirates into space with a grenade. You got one hell of a kill count already!" says Sparrow.

Robin's eyes water and she turns away. As a reward for his crass comment, Sparrow gets a slap to the back of the head from Ibis. Meanwhile, Blackbird turns Robin to him, puts his hand on her shoulder, and looks into her shaky, wet eyes.

"You don't have to kill anybody else. Just spray the area to keep them down while me and Ibis take care of them. But the more of us that are fighting, the better chance we have of repelling the pirates," says Blackbird.

"But–"

Blackbird puts his other hand on her shoulder and squeezes.

"Robin, please. I know you're scared, but I need your help. Will you help us?" says Blackbird softly.

After some seconds of pause, Robin gulps and nods, and Blackbird returns the nod.

"Thank you," says Blackbird.

Then there is Sparrow. He is swinging his rifle left to right and making shooting sounds. When he is done, he giggles and looks at Ibis with the rifle pointed at his gut and his finger on the trigger.

"This is nice. I feel so cool with it," says Sparrow.

Ibis slaps the rifle down. "That is not a toy!"

"I know that! But unlike Chickadee over there, I've played laser tag and paintball, so I know how these things work," says Sparrow.

Ibis shakes his head and goes to Blackbird.

"Are you ready?" asks Ibis.

Blackbird looks at Robin, and she keeps her rifle pointed down, her finger on the trigger guard, and has her safety on. She looks like she's going to be sick from anxiety overload.

"Yeah, we're ready as can be," says Blackbird.

That is when all the operational TV screens turn on, and Crow's voice flows through the speakers. The TVs that are not destroyed have Crow's face on them, and the ones with damaged screens are pixelated messes that occasionally flicker out.

"Ready as can be, eh?" says Crow. *"Let's see what we have here. We have Officer Impostor, leading a ragtag group consisting of a goat herder, a faggot, and some girl I vaguely recognize, and that's going to bug me until I figure out who you are."*

Ibis, Sparrow, and Blackbird look at Robin, and Robin's eyes dart between the camera and the group, somehow paler than before, and Sparrow gasps gleefully.

"Oh, this is going to be a juicy story," says Sparrow.

"So, since you guys decided it was fun to kill my pirates rather than cooperate, I've got a little gift for all of you."

The feed switches to *The City of Clouds* lobby from various angles, and they see the corpses of the security and the executed, but then the camera feeds switch to the interior of the businesses. One after another, civilians lay bunched at the doors and lying on the floor, dead. Eyes wide, bodies twisted, faces blue. One after the other, the same massacre.

Robin backs up, gasping. She puts her hand to her mouth, with tears streaking down her face and body trembling. Blackbird's jaw sets and he goes to the screen, breathing heavily, and Ibis' hands shake and his eyes widen.

"What have you done?" says Blackbird.

The nearby camera turns to Blackbird, and Crow's face returns with a stern expression.

"Did you think I was playing around, Officer Impostor?" says Crow. *"You killed my pirates. I wanted to keep things civil, but you and your friends just had to play hero, didn't you? Well, guess what! I killed these people without a second thought, and there are more locked in their rooms, locked in other businesses scattered around the ship. The more you resist me, the more people will die. Do you really want more blood on your hands? Do you really want to test me further?"*

Blackbird walks to the camera. On the screen, Crow leans forward, and Blackbird glares at the lens.

"You're a dead man, Crow. I swear to God, I will kill you," says Blackbird.

Crow stares for a few seconds, and then a wicked smile cracks on his face and he giggles.

"Good luck. God and man hasn't killed me yet," says Crow.

The screen switches to the emergency message, and the group looks at Blackbird. Ibis has a particular intensity.

Blackbird turns to the group. "We need to get to the air control and fast. If I can get in contact with the captain, he might be able to help us override the bridge control."

Blackbird walks past Robin, and the others follow him. But Robin stares at the emergency message on the screen, still in shock, heart heavy and breathing unsteady, with tears streaming down her face. Noticing that she hasn't moved, Blackbird stops and turns to her.

"Robin, we need to go," says Blackbird.

"Why did he do that?" whimpers Robin.

Ibis and Sparrow now look at Robin, and she trembles as she looks at Blackbird.

"Why did he kill them? If he wants us dead, why doesn't he just drain the air in our area?" asks Robin.

"Hey now, let's not get suicidal," says Sparrow.

"We should surrender! That'll save more lives, right?" says Robin.

"We can't surrender. They'll kill us if we do, and they'll get what they want and win, and do this to another habitat. We can't let that happen," says Ibis.

"But we got those people killed!" cries Robin, pointing at the screen. "That's blood on us!"

Blackbird walks to Robin and grabs the back of her head so he can look into her eyes.

"We didn't kill those people. He did," says Blackbird. "We didn't drain the air. He did. He's a psycho, Robin. He wants people to die. He's just trying to pass the blame on to us while he gets off on killing, and if we surrender and let him get away, he'll do this again. So, Ibis is right. We cannot let him escape."

"I, for one, am one hundred percent on board with getting rid of that guy," says Sparrow, grinning with his rifle aimed to the ceiling and finger on the trigger. "And you should be, too, Chickadee."

Robin looks at Sparrow, and seconds later she looks at Ibis.

"I'm in all the way," says Ibis.

Robin looks at Blackbird, and his hand slides down to her shoulder.

"Come on. I need you to fight. If not for us, do it for the ones Crow killed," says Blackbird.

Bellona's red tint is brightened by a brief flash of lightning that streaks across its bands and coils around its eye. Robin sniffles, wipes her eyes, smearing her makeup, and she nods.

"Okay," says Robin weakly. "Lead the way."

The Engine Cloud

A green-lit, thick metal door slides open with a loud **thud**. Ibis and Blackbird steps out sweeps the immediate area with their rifles raised. After they are a few steps in, Sparrow runs out and takes a knee, while snapping his rifle side to side and up and and down.

"Clear, Team Buttercup!" says Sparrow.

"How do you know this guy?" asks Blackbird to Ibis, jabbing his thumb at Sparrow.

"I took his hotel room when he didn't claim it. He's been a thorn in my side since," says Ibis.

Robin meekly follows the group. Her eyes widen and her jaw goes slack as she takes in the scenery of the Engine Cloud.

The area is a massive, hollowed-out orb with a network of walkways and railings. The light is dim for the most part, save for a few pockets from the clanking gears and humming turbines. Smaller lights blink, tubes of wires and fluids trace the curves of the orb, and in the center of it all is a large device with an hourglass shape. Its light is bright, even with the tinted materials surrounding it, . Mechanical arms with pointed tips are aimed at it, siphoning energy from it, which is then transferred to the wires and distributed around the ship.

Each walkway has a door, and numerous posters on metal slabs are placed evenly around the walkways. The posters depict safety advice, rules and regulations, and motivational posters, as well as maps and schematics. There are also gray, block-shaped panels connected to the tubes and mechanical arms.

"Alright, we're here," says Blackbird, his voice carrying in the large open space.

He does a quick read of one of the maps glued onto one of the metal platforms. After that, he looks around, and it takes him a minute to find the only yellow block with an assortment of levers and buttons surrounding screens of various sizes. It is connected to the thickest set of tubes that travel up the wall and split into the ceiling and the guts of the habitat. It is a few levels up, but it is in a good spot where they can see it clearly. Seeing this, Blackbird grins and runs over to the panel, while waving to the others to follow him.

"Over here!" shouts Blackbird.

The group follows him, with Robin close behind and Ibis staying in the back. When they reach the panel, Blackbird looks at the assortment of buttons and levers, and his smile drops.

"I have no idea what to do," says Blackbird.

"Are you serious? I thought you were a security guard," says Sparrow.

"I'm not. I just took the vest. Plus, what makes you think a security would know how to work a habitat engine?" says Blackbird.

"Do you think we can get in touch with the captain through the communicator?" asks Robin.

Blackbird and Sparrow look at her, and she shrugs.

"I mean, if the captain was dead, Crow would have bragged about it. So maybe there's an emergency line we can use?" says Robin.

Blackbird thinks for a moment, and activates his communicator and scrolls through a list of numbers on his wrist-top computer until he comes across a place labeled "Captain's Suit."

He dials the number and the communicator projects an audio box from the device on his shoulder. The group watches as a phone icon wiggles, with a pleasant ringing noise to go with it.

*****

In the Captain's Suit, Jay Azure is feeding his fish while his guards pace around, anticipating the trouble to come to their door.

"My God, these pirates are killing everyone," says a guard.

"Why haven't they drained our air yet?" asks another guard.

"They want me to suffer," says Jay. He sprinkles the last of his fish food in the tank. "The protection of the habitat is my responsibility, and they are using these executions as psychological warfare. With all the damages and lawsuits that'll come... that's going to be mildly inconvenient for me financially, but socially it is going to be a lifelong nightmare."

Jay sighs heavily, grabs a bottle of alcohol, and sits on a couch. He pops the lid off and chugs straight from the bottle, finishing with a loud gasp.

"If I had known this was going to happen, I would have let the other guy win and not rig the election," says Jay sadly. "Sure, I would still lose money, but I would be spared of the responsibilities of all the deaths."

Some of his guards nod in agreement, and a phone on the wall rings, displaying a number and *"Officer Blackwell Swan."*

"Sir! We're getting a call from a security officer!" says the guard near the phone.

"What?" Jay gets up and looks at the phone, and he grins from ear to ear and hurries to it. "This is great! We have a chance to retake the habitat!"

*****

Back in the Engine Cloud, the group is still waiting for someone to answer their communicator at various degrees of patience. Sparrow is checking his fingernails; Blackbird is tapping his foot; Ibis is looking around; and Robin is nibbling her lip and wringing her hands. Then there is a click, and an audio box replaces the phone icon.

*"Officer Blackwell Swan! So good to hear from you! This is your **real** captain speaking,"* says Jay.

"Uh, yeah, sorry to burst your bubble, but Officer Swan is dead. I just took his stuff to fight the pirates," says Blackbird.

There is a moment of silence, and then... *"You must be the troublemaker then. Officer Impostor as they say. You do realize you not surrendering has gotten a lot of people killed, right? I could sue you for damages and have you thrown in prison."*

Blackbird frowns and paces in a circle. "I've been doing more work getting rid of these pirates than you have, but feel free to sue and imprison me."

"Spicy fellow, aren't you?"

"Look, we need to be quick. I'm in the Engine Cloud trying to take control of the air supply, and I have no idea what to do," says Blackbird.

There is a moment of silence, and then one of the nearby cameras turns to them.

"Ah, I see you now," says Jay. *"You have Sparrow and Ibis with you, and that fine young lady. Then there's you. We've all met, now we're all working together! How cinematic."*

"We need to hurry. How do we get control of the air supply?" asks Blackbird.

"Alright, I'll help you. But you're going to have to let go of Swan's badge for a little while," says Jay.

"Why?" asks Blackbird.

"Because you're going to be on guard duty with Ibis since you two can handle weapons better than Sparrow and the fashionista can. So, you and Ibis shoot the pirates, and Sparrow and Robin can handle the easy task. Got it?" says Jay.

Blackbird sighs heavily and looks at Sparrow and Robin.

"Also, give the lucky winner your communicator," says Jay.

Blackbird reluctantly removes the communicator and extends his hand to Sparrow. His offer is quickly rejected with a frantic hand wave.

"Oh no, I'm not taking that responsibility," says Sparrow.

"What happened with being one hundred percent on board with stopping Crow?" asks Blackbird sourly.

"I lied. I'm more thirty-five percent," says Sparrow.

Robin holds her hand out to Blackbird.

"I'll take it," says Robin.

Blackbird begrudgingly clips the communicator onto Robin while giving Sparrow the stink eye. When it is attached, Robin's ear is filled with Jay's voice, and the wavelengths in his audio box fluctuate with his words.

"Ooh, I got lucky. Can you hear me, little lady?" asks Jay.

"I can hear you. And please call me Robin," says Robin.

"No problem, Robin. Your voice is just as good over the communicator as it is in person."

Robin nibbles her lip nervously and Blackbird frowns, gives Robin his badge, and goes to the edge to scan the area with Ibis.

"Okay, down to business," says Jay. *"Go to the control panel."*

Robin goes to the control panel.

"Slide the badge in the slot above the control levers."

Robin complies, and the lights flash yellow, and a small screen pops up with a menu.

"I see a menu," says Robin.

"Go to air supply and look for administrative override," says Jay.

Robin does this quickly, and schematics appear with multiple notes showing more rooms drained of oxygen. Robin's eyes widen, and her gut twists into a knot. She counts five rooms in total.

"Crow drained three more rooms!" says Robin.

"That's right, I did!" says Crow over the speakers. *"You guys just don't want to stop, so I'll make sure there's nobody left for you to save! And since you decided to talk to Captain Azure, I'm thinking I'm going to have a word with him personally for aiding enemies of my crew. What do you think about that, Captain?"*

"Eh. You know where I am, so come on over when you're ready," says Jay.

Meanwhile, Blackbird goes to the railing to glare at the camera.

"Killing you is going to be a pleasure, Crow," says Blackbird.

Gunshots suddenly ring out, and Robin shrieks and ducks down by the panel, and Ibis and Blackbird return fire.

"Pirates at seven!" yells Ibis.

"Sparrow, cover us!" says Blackbird while he ducks from a stream of bullets that damage the railing and destroy warning posters.

Sparrow runs forward, screaming like a shrill, high-pitched banshee and shooting wildly. Bullets ricochet off the railings and walls. Lights break, pirates duck, and Ibis and Blackbird run to cover.

"You wanted to be heroes, right? Well, the newly dead civilians are happy for you!" says Crow.

Meanwhile, Robin pokes her head up and watches Ibis and Blackbird moving to new locations, and Sparrow running down a flight of stairs to avoid a hail of bullets directed towards him. He's still screaming and shooting wildly.

"*Robin are you with me?*" asks Jay.

"I–I'm here," says Robin.

"*Go to administrative override.*"

Robin stays close to the panel and flinches as the bullets fly near her. Some of them strike the hourglass-shaped engines, creating crackles and flashes of light. She does quick work, finding what she needs to. Two password and voice command prompts appear.

"I'm in. There's two passwords and a voice command prompt," says Robin.

"*Password is going to be all lower case, no spaces. Igloo penguins, number 4, the win. Exclamation mark. Second password will be all caps-lock. Burrito annihilation, eight-eight, period.*"

Robin types in the passwords.

"Done," says Robin.

"*Alright, now lean close so you are practically kissing the panel and tell me when you've hit the record button,*" says Jay.

Screams of death and curses mix with the gunfire, and Robin looks over her shoulder to see Ibis fighting pirates. He slams one's neck into the railing, slashes another pirate's face with his knife, and uses his pistol to gun down a third one, before finishing off the second target.

Blackbird is running and gunning, and leaps over the railing to kick a pirate off from the lower level. They tumble out of view, and–

"*Robin are you there?*" says Jay.

"I'm here!" Robin leans over and hits a red button next to the voice command box. "Go!"

"*Peter Piper picked a peck of pickled peppers. A peck of pickled peppers Peter Piper picked. If Peter Piper picked a peck of pickled peppers, where's the peck of pickled peppers Peter Piper picked?*"

"**Access Granted,**" says a friendly computer voice. "**Welcome, Captain Jay Horus Azure.**"

Robin laughs, then flinches as a stream of bullets fly behind her and hit the hourglass engines. There is another flare and crackle of electricity, and Jay's feed almost cuts out. It quickly recovers, and the menu has everything bright green, with Jay's name in the corner.

"It worked! I'm in!" says Robin.

"Good. Now hit emergency lockout for the air. That will lock them out," says Jay.

Robin hits that, and a message appears:

Bridge still in use. Do you wish to continue? Y/N

Robin hits "Y" and follows with returning the air to rooms that are blinking red.

*****

Crow is rolling and squeezing his stress ball and watching as more bodies drop in another room, as the civilians struggle to breathe and claw at their doors. Then his computer beeps, and on the camera feeds, he sees air rushing back into the rooms. He scowls and types on the computers, but all he has are error messages.

"Oh..." Crow switches the camera feed and sees Robin at the control panel. He growls and squeezes his stress ball. "Oh... *You.* You... Man, you are going to bug me."

*****

In the Engine Cloud, Robin laughs and bounces on her feet as the message shows the bridge being locked out and air being returned to the rooms.

"I did it! Crow doesn't have control over the air anymore!" says Robin.

"Very good. Please return the communicator to Officer Impostor and don't die. I still want to date you," says Jay.

Robin removes the badge and puts it in her pocket. "Right. Of course. Thank you for your help, Captain Azure."

"No. Thank you."

Jay's feed cuts out, and suddenly the intercom dings.

"ATTENTION PIRATES! CAN SOMEBODY PLEASE KILL THE HOT CHICK BY

THE CONTROL PANEL! THANK YOU!" screams Crow.

And right after Crow says this, bullets strike near Robin. She shrieks and scrambles for cover, accidentally knocking a lever up along the way. She crouches down and covers her head, but much to her confusion, the whirring in the Engine Cloud gets louder.

The confusion shifts to worry as the hourglass-shaped machines glow brighter with crackles of electricity tugging on the air. The rush of energy makes Robin's hair stand up, and her group, plus the pirates, look around nervously.

"Robin, what did you do?" says Blackbird, while struggling to keep a pirate from stabbing him.

A sudden force yanks Robin away from the platform and everyone else flies off their feet. She screams and grabs the grated floor, but her skin tears on the floor and her bloody fingers slip out. She screams again and skids along the floor, until she grabs a railing and wraps herself around it.

Sparrow shrieks and is pressed against a metal wall holding a safety poster.

Pirates roll and bounce across the walkways, with some hitting the railing, spinning out of control and falling out of sight, or being cooked when they hit the hourglass machines.

Blackbird and Ibis wrestle with their respective pirates. Ibis turns his pirate to a railing and smashes their spine and neck against it. He digs his fingers into the floor grate while his other hand holds the railing.

Blackbird turns his pirate and slams them into the floor, before being hit by another pirate taking advantage of the momentum. The two tumble, and Blackbird kicks the pirate off and grabs a railing while the pirate rolls away.

Warning lights and alarms flash throughout the Engine Cloud and–

*****

In the Aqua Storage Cloud, warning lights swirl and reflect off the ice, and the pirates grab what they can while the habitat zooms through space. The tube connecting their ship suddenly snaps, and the decompression launches pirates, carts, and debris into space.

The hole gets bigger as blocks of ice and machinery hit the hull, and the hijacked water ship spins out of control with a gaping hole in its side, spinning out debris, more pirates, and rapidly freezing water.

*****

At the vault, Nightingale holds on to a bolted-down table as she struggles to stay put. Loose equipment bounces around, striking the pirates, and Talon clings to his drill while cursing up a storm.

*****

In a stairwell, the sudden force of momentum knocks Raven off her feet and presses her into the wall. She screams as the g-force presses down on her, making her equipment dig into her. Out of the corner of her eye, she sees the door leading to the Aqua Storage Cloud flash to red with a warning of a hull breach.

"Oh crap," groans Raven.

*****

Oro and his pirates tumble across the floor of the Communications Cloud. The room is a round chamber with a pillar of cubes extending to the ceiling. A ring of computers surrounds the pillar, but some are broken as pirates bounce around and break their spines, necks, and heads on railing and equipment, leading to some being electrocuted to the point of bursting into flames.

A projector labeled as "Bellona Map" is near the pillar. Oro hits it and bounces off to hit a railing. His impact causes the projector to spark and reboot with a wide variety of conflicting messages.

*****

On the bridge, Crow tightly holds on to his chair while his pirates are flung about. Some go limp when they crash against the bridge equipment and others skid across the floor, desperately trying to grab what they can.

*****

In the Captain's Suit, Jay holds on to a rail and watches in horror as his aquariums shatter, sending small tidal waves of glass and pebble-filled water surging across the floor, taking his fish and their aquarium decorations with him. Bottles of alcohol fall loose and shatter on the floor, and his guards shout while they struggle to hold on to anything they can while avoiding the shard-infested water.

*****

Back in the Engine Cloud, Blackbird kicks another pirate away. The pirate tumbles and hits a wall, and Blackbird grits his teeth and climbs the railing.

"Shut it off!" shouts Blackbird.

Robin reaches out with a bloody hand and grabs the next piece of railing. She strains her limbs and core to pull herself up. Her muscles and bones are in pain fighting against the momentum, but she keeps going. One. Section. At. A. Time.

Bloody hand prints are smeared on the railing, and tears streak down Robin's face as her fingers burn from the cuts. When she finally reaches the control panel, she pulls the lever down.

The engines shut off, but *The City of Clouds* keeps going and the warning lights and alarms stay active, so Robin hits the stabilizers. The small engines positioned around the habitat turn on, launching in bursts to reduce the structure's speed.

The habitat's speed gradually decreases, and everyone collapses in a heap, panting and wheezing, or cursing.

Ibis rests against the railing, shaking, and looking at his bloody fingers. Blackbird wobbles and uses the railing for support. Sparrow falls to the floor. Robin slumps down, crying and looking at her torn fingers, bloody palms, and ruined gloves.

"M–My gloves are ruined," sniffles Robin. "My gloves. My skin. THEY'RE FLABBY!"

The flesh on her fingertips is tattered, and she screams as the burning, sharp pain surges through. She's sure she can see her bones, too.

Bullets start flying again, and Blackbird and Ibis swear up a storm as they shoot back, but Robin can only stare at her mangled fingers.

However, she snaps out of it when bullets strike near her. She screams and scurries away on her fists and knees to escape the chaos. Bullets ricochet off the railing and floor, and sparks fly from equipment being destroyed.

As she crawls, Sparrow rushes next to her and helps her up. "Come on, this way!"

The two run to a break room, and Sparrow sits Robin on a chair and rummages through cabinets marked with a red cross. Robin stares at her shredded fingers, whimpering and shivering. She feels nauseous looking at the ripped flesh and the blood coating her hand and wrists, now dripping to the floor. Yet she can't look away either.

When Sparrow returns, he removes Robin's gloves, exposing a three-diamond tattoo on her hand. He sprays hydrochloride on Robin's fingers. She yelps and yanks her hands away, flicking bubbling blood on herself and Sparrow, but he pulls her hand to him and wraps her fingers in gauze and medical tape. Then he moves on to the next hand and repeats it.

"There. All done. Now you owe me," says Sparrow.

"That's fine. What do you want in return?" winces Robin.

She stares at her bandaged fingers, which are throbbing, and Sparrow hums and taps his chin.

"I don't know... Maybe a better fashion sense?" says Sparrow.

Robin looks at Sparrow sharply, and he smirks and waves his fingers at Robin's ruined clothes.

"Your taste is just ugly," says Sparrow.

Robin frowns. "Criticize my fashion sense all you want, but at least I don't look like I killed a neon tiger and used the cheapest tailor on the market to make a clearance rack special!"

"Puh-*leeze*," scoffs Sparrow. "This fabric is fabulous. And for the record, it wasn't on the clearance rack. I used a twenty percent coupon. Clearance racks are for plebs."

Robin rolls her eyes. Then the door opens, and Ibis and Blackbird enter, both panting and sweating, and covered in their blood and the blood of their enemies. Robin hastily puts her gloves back on, and Ibis keeps an eye outside, keeping the door from closing by placing his foot in front of the sensor while Blackbird goes to Robin.

"Are you okay?" asks Blackbird.

Robin nods, and Blackbird kneels in front of her and inspects her hands. After that, he looks at Sparrow.

"Thanks for helping her," says Blackbird.

"It's because I want Chickadee to live," says Sparrow.

"Oh, so you do care about someone," says Ibis.

"Don't be snarky. I care about all of you."

Ibis grunts, and Blackbird removes the communication set from Robin's shoulder and ear, and she returns the badge to him. After that, he turns on the communicator, bringing up Jay's audio box.

"Captain, we secured the air and got the engine under control," says Blackbird.

"Good... Good. All it cost was my fish and alcohol," says Jay.

Blackbird frowns and Ibis shakes his head. He's not mad, just disappointed that he isn't surprised by Jay's words.

"I'm sorry about your fish!" says Robin loudly.

"It's fine. Fish are replaceable. And I'd rather the fish be dead than me," says Jay.

"Hang tight, Captain. We're almost done with the pirates. We just need to get to the communications section to send out an SOS," says Blackbird.

"Be sure to kill Crow, too. That guy's a douche bag," says Jay. *"And if you do kill him, I'll give you a handsome reward."*

"Believe me, I plan on it. With or without a reward," says Blackbird.

"Good. Call me when you need me again."

"Will do."

The audio box disappears, and Blackbird sighs, stands up, and looks at the group.

"Everyone okay?" asks Blackbird.

The group nods and vocally acknowledges Blackbird, and Ibis adjusts his stance and rifle.

"The area is still clear. We should move while we still can," says Ibis.

"Right. Let's go," says Blackbird.

Blackbird helps Robin up, and the group quickly leaves the room.

*****

Back at the vault, Nightingale stands up, groaning, bruised, and bloodied. The other pirates are in similar states, but all of them are recovering in a timely manner.

"What the hell was that?" says Nightingale.

Crow's audio box appears in front of her, but the projection is weak and flickering.

"Love are you okay?" asks Crow.

"Yeah," winces Nightingale. "I believe we got four more of the security pylons deactivated."

"Good. When you get the money, make your way to the lifeboats. That flashy girl turned on the engines and decoupled our ride."

Nightingale sighs heavily and wipes her face. "Shit... Alright. We'll have to make it quick then. Lifeboats aren't exactly the best ships around."

"Our main ship is nearby, so we won't be in those boats for long. But hurry up and get the money. This habitat is cursed."

"Got it."

Crow's audio box disappears, and Nightingale rolls her neck and shoulders and goes to Talon.

"Back to work. The rest of you, clean this up!" orders Nightingale.

The pirates scramble to complete the cleanup, and Talon resumes drilling.

*****

In the Communications Cloud, Oro A. Guila groans and curses under his breath as he uses the railing for support. His impact bent it and left him with a headache. He looks around and sees many of his pirates are dead, and the room is wrecked with broken terminals and sparking equipment.

However, there are still a good number of pirates left, but they are a bit discombobulated. They stagger and curse as they regain their bearings, and Oro growls and clenches his fists as he paces in a circle, taking in the carnage.

"What the hell was that?" says Oro to himself.

A nearby camera turns to him, and an audio box is projected from his communicator.

"Oro, can you hear me?" asks Crow.

"I can," says Oro.

"That hot chick put the habitat in super speed. It caused a mess, and I'm really pissed-off right now, so if you could do me a favor and kill her, that would be great!" says Crow.

"Consider it done."

Oro disconnects before Crow can say anything else. Then he grabs a rifle and orders his group to follow him as he leaves the room.

The Communications Cloud

After achieving their goal at the Engine Cloud, the group quickly made it to the Communications Cloud; thanks to the lack of pirates harassing them the trip was peaceful. However, fear lingers in them. They don't know where the pirates are hiding and all silently felt the fear of pirates waiting for them on the other side of the Communications Cloud's door.

When the group reaches the Communications Cloud, Blackbird uses his badge to free the emergency door lever. He looks at Ibis, and Ibis steadies his rifle. Robin stands next to Blackbird and copies Ibis, while Sparrow stays back and watches the pathway.

Blackbird takes a deep breath, pulls the lever, and the door slides open.

Robin and Ibis peek in but see nothing.

"Stay there," orders Ibis to Robin.

Robin nods, and Ibis slides in, weapon raised and sweeping the area. While he does this, Robin looks at Sparrow. He is pretending to shoot at people again.

"Clear!" calls Ibis.

"Hallway is clear here, my dears," says Sparrow.

"Very funny. Get in here," says Blackbird.

Robin goes in with Blackbird, and her eyes widen with wonder while Blackbird helps Ibis inspect the area further.

The chamber is round with a pillar of cubes extending to the ceiling. A ring of computers surrounds it, and railings separate the computers from the rest of the area. Cameras are placed in strategic locations, there are terminals lining the wall, and a projector labeled as "Bellona Map" is near the pillar.

Said projector is currently stuck on displaying a loading image comprised of Bellona spinning, with a ticking clock in the middle.

Seeing this makes Robin's brain click to the rest of the mess.

The computers surrounding the pillar are damaged, with cracked screens and broken keyboards. The railing is bent, the terminals are smashed with dead (and electrically burnt) pirates laying in front of them, and their weapons are scattered.

Ibis and Blackbird retrieve ammo and medical supplies from the dead, and Sparrow walks in, whistling.

"Wow. What a mess," says Sparrow.

"What happened here?" asks Robin, looking at a pirate whose head was smashed into the wall.

"You probably killed them when you put the habitat on super speed," says Blackbird.

"Oh..." Robin gasps. "Oh! Oh, dear... I... I..."

Robin paces in circles, muttering and tugging at her hair, and Sparrow snorts a laugh.

"Wow. Chickadee is good at accidentally killing people," says Sparrow.

"And that's not good!" cries Robin. "I want to have a husband and children, but if I'm good at accidentally killing people, what if I accidentally kill them? What if I start accidentally killing more people and become a serial manslaughterer?"

Blackbird shakes his head, and Robin goes to the other end of the room, tightly gripping the railing.

"I think I'll stay over here for a while. You guys will be safer if I'm not next to you," says Robin.

"So far you have only accidentally killed those who wished to harm us, so I think we're safe," says Ibis.

"I'm not risking it," says Robin.

"Alright, if that makes you feel better, I won't bug you about it. As for me, I'm going to watch the entrance while all of you do your own thing," says Ibis.

"I'll work on the communications," says Blackbird. "And Sparrow?"

Sparrow smiles thinly at Blackbird.

"Go stand with Ibis," says Blackbird.

"Why? I can be useful for something," says Sparrow.

"Like what?"

"Providing moral support."

"Give Ibis moral support. I don't need any."

Sparrow huffs, goes over to Ibis, who is now by the door, and leans against the door frame with a fake smile.

"So, how's it going, Aladdin?" asks Sparrow.

Ibis looks away, and Sparrow snickers.

"Come on, don't be like that," says Sparrow.

Ibis tries to ignore him.

"Do you think you'll be open for an interview when this is all over?" asks Sparrow.

"When this is all over, I'm going to retire from this and work at a nursery," says Ibis.

"Ah, the place where you groom plants to a ripe age before ripping them out by the roots and selling them off for profit!"

Ibis stares at Sparrow with disgust. Sparrow grins. Ibis stares at him for another few seconds before slowly looking away. Sparrow tries to look at his eyes, but Ibis does everything he can to not look at Sparrow.

"Come on, that was funny!" says Sparrow.

"Stop talking to me," says Ibis.

"Never." Sparrow looks at Blackbird and Robin. "What do you think they're talking about?"

Back at the pillar, Robin passes a ladder on a rail, and she looks at a broken computer. Behind her, the projection's loading screen switches to a map of Bellona and *The City of Clouds'* location. It is currently near the moon Bellona-45 (a.k.a. Rebecca the Ice Queen). Robin notices the change due to the light reflecting off the metal changing, and when she turns around, she tilts her head at the projector.

Rebecca the Ice Queen orbits closely to Bellona-44 (a.k.a. Steve). Both moons have multiple glowing dots on them. Rebecca also has an error message above it.

Robin pokes Rebecca and the moon enlarges, and with it, more details displaying mining locations and bio-domes, as well as orbiting stations.

"Hey Blackbird, there's an error message for Rebecca," says Robin.

Blackbird goes to the projection and scrunches his brow.

"That's an ice mining moon," says Blackbird. "It's safe to say they are responsible for bringing *The City of Clouds* their water. Habitats run a tight ship when it comes to water and food supplies. And with the celebration today, they must have special ordered... water..."

Blackbird's voice drifts away, and after a few seconds of stillness, he bursts into great speed and starts frantically trying to get the computers to turn on. He taps the power buttons, flicks their switches, kicks them, smacks them, yells at them; and the whole time Robin stares at him blankly.

"Uh, Blackbird?" says Robin.

"The pirates had to have hijacked an ice ship! That's got to be how they got in," says Blackbird. He presses the power button and presses his ear against a computer. Nothing. "The ice station is probably asking about the ice ship, and if they are asking about the ice ship, then it would be proof that the pirates used an ice ship to sneak in!"

"Really?"

"Well, we'd still have to check cameras and do witness testimonies if they left survivors, but it would fortify my hunch if they're asking about the ice ship."

"How many times can you say, 'ice ship' in a minute?" says Sparrow loudly.

Blackbird snaps to Sparrow. "Not now!"

Sparrow holds up his hand. "Hey, I'm just trying to lighten the mood."

Blackbird hurries around the pillar, mumbling irritably to himself while putting on his headphones and listening to music. As he does this, a camera turns to him, and his communicator projects the audio box.

"Hey, Officer Impostor, what's going on down there?" asks Jay.

Blackbird moodily removing his headphones.

"I just got started," grumbles Blackbird.

"What's going on down there?" repeats Jay.

"The communications room is wrecked. We can't get an SOS out," says Blackbird.

"So, what makes you think kicking and whacking computers will make them turn on?"

Blackbird doesn't reply.

"That's what I thought. Anyway, the good news is that I can help you get the SOS out. From my end, it looks like there's a blockade of some kind, but it'll be easy to override. All it needs is a system reboot." The cameras in the room adjust their lenses. *"We're going to have to hurry, though. I don't know how many pirates Crow has left, but I can help you get the communications system back online, and then you can send out an SOS to Nyx. They send aid and we go to Andromeda to get pampered for our troubles."*

"Nyx? That planet is off-limits. There shouldn't be anyone on there!" says Blackbird.

"As of now it is the closest military installation. The planet is almost perfectly aligned with Bellona at this point, so they'll be able to reach us faster. Now, step one. Give the communicator to Robin."

"Robin!" calls Blackbird.

Robin looks at Blackbird and her eyes snap to the communicator when he holds it out to her.

"The captain wants to talk to you again," says Blackbird.

Robin hesitantly grabs the communicator and clips it to her body.

"Can you hear me?" asks Jay.

"I can," replies Robin.

"Good. We got some work to do, and your hands are smaller than the sausages you're with, which means you'll have an easier time dealing with the equipment up there," says Jay.

Robin looks at her bandaged fingers. "My fingers are damaged."

"Too bad. We need you to do this. There's a ladder that goes to the top of the pillar. At the top of the pillar is a panel marked with a spiral and three-oh-three. You open it, and there's a handle that you can turn. Normally, maintenance has a device they use, but we don't have time to look for them or the tool. So, get climbing!"

Robin sighs and climbs the ladder. Her face twitches from the little bites of pain on her fingers. As she climbs, one of the cameras turns to her and the lens adjusts. When she reaches the top, she finds the panel and sees that it needs a flathead screwdriver. Rather than climbing back down to look for one, she pulls out her room key card and uses it to unscrew the panel. It is slow and awkward, but it gets the job done.

"So, where do you want to go for our first date when this is all over?" asks Jay.

Robin frowns and works with greater speed, and Blackbird tilts his head slightly.

"Can we get back to the thing?" asks Robin.

"Sure, no problem. But I am curious about something. How come you never returned my messages? Was I too old?" says Jay.

"They're behind a paywall!"

"You get five free messages."

"Per month. And for your information, I just use dating apps to kill time because some jerk named Seagull4Winz, aka Cliff, stood me up, so I don't even know why I use them! Dating apps suck! They're terrible, addictive, money and soul sucking black holes of despair!" says Robin.

Ibis cringes, and Sparrow gasps loudly and points at him.

"Hey, everybody! Ibis just had a weird reaction!" shouts Sparrow.

"Sparrow, you dick!" snaps Ibis.

Robin, Blackbird, and Jay's camera turn to Ibis.

"Why'd you have a weird reaction?" asks Jay.

Ibis sighs heavily and bangs his head against the door frame. "I was Seagull4Winz... I was Cliff Birdie," says Ibis.

The whole room goes quiet. Even the machinery seems to lose some noise, and Robin narrows her eyes at him.

"What?" says Robin heavily.

"Yeah... I was Cliff. I stood you up. And I signed you up for the lottery under Sparrow's suggestion."

The group looks at Sparrow, and he holds up his hands.

"Hey, in my defense, I didn't know it was you. He just said, 'some girl'," says Sparrow.

"Some girl, huh?" says Robin sourly, glaring at Ibis with hot tears burning her eyes.

Ibis forces himself to look at Robin. "I signed you up for the vacation lottery because I felt terrible about what I did."

"You mean you felt bad about pretending to be an entirely different person and then standing me up?" says Robin.

Ibis nods. "Yeah. I knew that if I showed up as me and not Cliff, then you would freak out. I never thought it would go as far as it did. So, I ended it before I hurt you even more. Also, I was never going to make it because I was on my way to Oros for an assignment."

"Oh my God," groans Robin. She bangs her head on the pillar. Slow. And. Hard. Tears soak her cheeks, and her body trembles while her throat tightens. "This is the worst day ever!"

Robin snaps her glare back to Ibis and points at him; blood is once again seeping past the bandages on her fingers.

"I am here on this ship on this messed-up day because of you! You made me miserable twice!" screams Robin.

"It wasn't supposed to be like this! I'm sorry about all this. None of this should have happened! But when we get out of here, I'll make it up to you, I promise!" says Ibis.

"You can make it up to me by never contacting me or being in my proximity again," says Robin.

Robin resumes her work, the group stays silent, and Sparrow pats Ibis's shoulder sympathetically. A few seconds later, Robin suddenly looks at Ibis with a fire in her eyes.

"What the hell is wrong with you, anyway?" yells Robin.

This makes the group jump, and Ibis wince.

"Do you get a kick out of pretending to be hot, muscular, blonde hair, blue-eyed, chiseled sculptor of a man to seduce female products?" says Robin.

Blackbird tilts his head questionably at Robin.

"No! But for the record, I got banned and blacklisted for using fake images," says Ibis shamefully.

"*Serves you right for getting banned. There's a reason why the TOS has **real*** *photos in there. It is for the safety of the user base. A lot of weirdos are out there. Now your lies have hurt poor Robin's feelings,"* says Jay.

Meanwhile, Robin resumes her work with a red face and body quivering as she breathes heavily.

"Uh... Robin? Are you okay?" asks Blackbird.

"Great. Just great," says Robin. She snaps at Ibis again. "Do you realize how hard it is to find a blonde-haired, blue-eyed human?"

The group looks at Ibis, his brows scrunched in thought.

"I... uh, I imagine it is difficult?" says Ibis uneasily.

"They're less than one percent of the human population!" says Robin. "They're like a genetic trophy!"

"Nice," says Blackbird sourly.

Robin waves her hand at Blackbird. "I didn't mean it like that. You're special in your own way.... Hold on, you're not even blonde! Why are you offended?"

"My adopted father's blonde."

"This is gold. Keep going, Chickadee," giggles Sparrow.

"No. I'm done. I'm sorry, Blackbird, that was offensive of me. But I need to get this thing taken care of so you guys can do the thing you need to do. No more distractions!" says Robin.

"I know this going to sound a bit strange, but if you're that concerned about that particular breed of human, then petition the government to use our cloning technology to mass produce them," says Ibis.

"They'll lose their specialty if we did that," says Robin.

"Okay, fine. Why not order a clone then?" suggests Sparrow.

"That's an idea. They're cheaper than they used to be. And the payment plan system means they are affordable for anyone in an upper middle-class income," says Jay.

Ibis and Sparrow nod and murmur in agreement, Blackbird rolls his eyes, and Robin's jaw drops.

"Did you not hear me?" snaps Robin. "There's nothing special about clones! We're just mass-produced, easily disposable products built from subjects who volunteered their genetic code and brain scans!"

"We?" says Blackbird.

"Forget it!" snaps Robin.

Robin snaps back to the panel, finishing removing the last screws, and she pries it open with her bloody fingers. Inside the pillar cube is a network of switches, wires, and cords around a small, locked, red dial, all illuminated by a single bulb.

"Jay, what do I need to do?" asks Robin.

"I thought you were familiar in another way. Rosalina Rosewood clone model, right?" asks Jay. *"I personally agree with Ibis on this. Let's clone a bunch of blondes. And redheads. We need more gingers! Or cross breed them to make blonde-ginger clones! I have enough influence; I can start a petition. My treat for you helping me retake my habitat."*

"Like a strawberry blonde thing? I can dig it," says Sparrow.

"Jay, we're wasting time," says Robin irritably.

"Alright, alright. Relax," says Jay. *"There should be a dial. It is locked, but some muscle should break the lock. After you break it, turn the dial counterclockwise. That will reboot the system. After that, it will ask for a password and voice command, which is where I will come in."*

Robin reaches in and grunts as she twists the dial. Her fingers pulse, burn, and ache, and blood drips on the wires. After a minute of struggling, the dial suddenly twists with a loud snap, and Robin turns it counterclockwise.

The computers down below hum and flicker to life. Some are a mess of colors and cracks, others don't even turn on, but one is in good condition, and Blackbird immediately goes to it.

"Alright, get down here! We have one working computer," says Blackbird.

"That's all we need," says Jay.

Robin begins her descent, but her hands tremble, and her muscles are tense to keep her from slipping due to her blood seeping past her bandages and wetting the bars.

"Okay, now that I am done, is there *anybody* on this ship that hasn't seen my dating profiles?" says Robin as she climbs down.

Sparrow raises his hand. "Me. But it's only because I hate women."

"Why?" asks Ibis.

"They're nasty creatures, and they get all bloaty and weird and mean and will stab you in the neck with a fork if you say the wrong thing."

Robin finishes climbing down and looks at her bloody fingers.

"Does someone have fresh bandages I can use? My fingers hurt and I don't want blood staining my clothes," says Robin sourly.

Blackbird takes out some bandages from his pouch, removes Robin's broken bandages, and treats her wounded fingers. After Blackbird finishes re-bandaging Robin's fingers, he looks at Sparrow.

"So, you're gay because a woman on her period stabbed you in the neck with a fork?" says Ibis.

Sparrow laughs. "No, it started after I cleaned the woman's room at a Hearty's Junior." He takes a deep, whimsical breath and looks at the ceiling. "I was seventeen at the time..."

"Nobody cares," says Jay.

Sparrow scoffs. "The nerve of you."

"Yeah, Sparrow. None of us give a shit about your shitty toilet adventure. We have work to do," says Blackbird. "Captain, hurry up with Robin so I can have my stuff back."

"Alright, hold your pigeons," says Jay. *"Robin, time for the next phase."*

Robin goes to the properly operating computer. She quickly brings up the menu and goes through the options until she gets to a password screen.

"Password?" asks Robin.

"Number 'eight.' Capital 'D.' Lower case o-g-s. Symbol, plus sign. Capital 'P.' Lowercase l-a-y-i-n-g. Capital 'P.' Number zero. Capital 'K.. Lowercase e-r. Symbol, exclamation mark. Numbers one-niner-oh-three."

Robin types in the password, and the screen changes to a voice command box. Robin sets it up and positions herself so that the communicator is close to the microphone, and she has her finger aimed at the recording button.

"I'm ready,'" says Robin.

"Hit it," says Jay.

Robin hits the button and–

"When a doctor doctors a doctor, does the doctor doing the doctoring doctor as the doctor being doctored wants to be doctored or does the doctor doing the doctoring doctor as he wants to doctor?" says Jay.

The computer beeps and a new screen appears. Robin keeps close to the microphone as she selects the emergency signal function and goes through the motions to set up a new message. When it is all said and done, she has her finger on the record button again.

"Alright, I'm ready to send out the signal," says Robin.

"Punch it," says Jay.

Robin hits the record button. "Go."

"Alpha-alpha-zero-niner-fury-ultima-bastion-alpha-red. Light-The City of Clouds-Bellona," says Jay swiftly. *"Alright, send it."*

Robin stops the recording, and the computer's screen gives a message acknowledging the signal has been created. Then she sends it out on loop, and smiles proudly while turning to the group.

"The signal is sent," says Robin.

"Good," says Blackbird. "Next stop. The bridge."

*****

Raven takes a deep breath and looks over the edge of the bridge in the Engine Cloud. The Engine Cloud is a giant, hollow orb with a lot of technological junk on the edges and weird hourglass-shaped machines in the center, with a lot of empty spaces. So, the network of pathways is really a network of bridges for Raven. And her anxiety is made worse by the dead pirates around her.

Blood and corpses are everywhere. Shot, stabbed, battered, rails bent, consoles smashed, a fan covered in blood; so many stories; so many pirates with painful ends.

Raven shudders, removes her backpack, and looks inside to inspect her collection of explosive bricks.

She stares at the explosives with a racing heart and shaky fingers. She swallows and wipes sweat off her brow, and then she seals it, opens another pouch on her backpack and pulls out a rope, a belt, and a pair of clips. She puts on the belt, clips the rope to the belt and railing, and slips the backpack on so that it is on her chest. She grips the railing and takes a deep breath.

"Sorry, *City*. But I got bills to pay," says Raven.

Then she begins her descent into the Engine Cloud.

Surprise!

Crow presses his stress ball against his head with one hand while the other digs into his scalp. The emergency signal has been broadcast and his monitor is not shy about alerting him. The worst part is that it should not have happened since Nightingale put a block in the system and the crew was poisoned. But then again, a part of him is not surprised that it has happened, since everything has gone wrong on this habitat.

This truly has been the worst raid ever.

Crow turns the camera to Nightingale's group. Their drilling has made progress, and members of their group are bandaged after that stunt what's-her-face pulled with the engines.

He's still agitated that he can't remember where he's seen her before, but her insane engine maneuver got him a lot of dead and injured pirates. And now that Crow thinks about it, with the way things have gone on *The City of Clouds*, a nagging feeling is tormenting his brain. It seems a little too easy for Captain Jay Azure to have his fortune sitting in a vault with only a few guards.

With that thought, Crow slides to another monitor, flips through the instruction manual, and after a quick read, he scrolls through the menu and finds logs. He goes through the repair logs and cross references repairs with the vault floor.

Nothing.

Crow frowns and rubs his chin while he squeezes the stress ball. He searches for the floor *above* the vault room and sees a repair log for floor repair and replacement. He selects it, and his eyes dart side to side, reading the notes and finding that cutting and welding equipment had been used to cut, replace, and cover an area four feet by three feet.

The location?

Directly above the vault.

"Oh shit," says Crow.

*****

The drill stops, and Talon smiles proudly as he retracts the dull and smoking drill bit.

"That's the last one," says Talon. "Some good twists should open the vault."

"Good," says Nightingale. She waves at the other pirates. "Get the bags ready! And you, open the vault."

The pirates hurry to set up the duffle bags. Talon stands up and wipes his sweaty hands on his pants before gripping the vault's spoke handle. He grunts as he twists it. Muted metallic pops and snaps echo from the large door, and Nightingale grins and rubs her hands.

Then Crow's audio box appears in front of her, still pixelated and fuzzing out.

"Love don't open the vault!" orders Crow.

Talon turns the spoke handle.

"Why not?" asks Nightingale.

"Because it's rigged!" yells Crow.

Nightingale looks at Talon. He is turning the spoke handle faster and there are multiple clicks.

"Wait! Stop!" orders Nightingale.

"We're almost there," says Talon.

The pirates shout encouragements and crowd around Talon, and Nightingale tries to push her way through the crowd.

"Stop! It's rigged!" yells Nightingale.

Talon pulls the door open, and a bright flash of light and fire and a wall of raw force throws Nightingale and the other pirates off their feet. Fire and shrapnel rip through the bodies and surrounding area.

The metal shards tear into Nightingale as she bounces down the hallway with torn flesh. Some pirates hit the walls and crumble in limp heaps, others land in burning pieces.

Nightingale rolls on her hands and knees, coughing and clutching her wounded side. She watches in horror as her pirates lay bleeding and dying, with Talon nothing more than a husk of shredded meat and broken bones.

Each of their voices get weaker, and Nightingale watches, short of breath and trembling, as mangled and gutted bodies slowly die in their pools of blood. Pockets of fire flicker on the destroyed corpses. Broken lights hang down, raining sparks and briefly lighting up the blood on the walls and floor. The cameras are destroyed, Nightingale's communicator is smashed, and the duffle bags are burning.

The vault door is wide open, with Talon's hand still clutching it.

Nightingale gets up on wobbly legs. She limps forward. Her broken sunglasses fall off, and when she reaches the vault, she drops to her knees and stares inside.

It's empty.

Nothing is on the shelves, and the floor has bits of detonated claymores.

"H-How? HOW!" cries Nightingale. She looks at the vault's ceiling and screams, "How the hell–"

Nightingale stops. Her eyes widen and her mouth falls open as tears roll down her burnt and bloodied face.

Seams of bubbled metal form a square in the ceiling.

Nightingale's breathing is still shaky, and her mouth hangs open while her eyes trace the metal.

"That bastard," gasps Nightingale. "That. Absolute. Fucking. Bastard!"

*****

On the bridge, Crow's mouth hangs open. His eyes cannot break away from the screen. Nightingale and her team were there and then disappeared in a flash of light. Now, all he has is an error message. His brain still isn't sure if he saw things right.

Then Jay's audio box appears, and he is laughing hysterically.

"Oh Crow! Crow Magnolia! Big. Bad. Pirate! I am so disappointed in you! Did you really think I would leave my money in a vault? Man, you suck!" taunts Jay.

Crow's hand trembles, and pieces of his stress ball fall to the floor, torn from his fingernails digging into it.

Jay laughs again. *"Listen to me. I know what you're doing. You're pointing at me. Blaming me. Hating me. Well, guess what? When you point at me, remember, you came here. In **my territory**. You wanted to **rob me**. You killed so many people for money that was **not yours**. That money is mine. And I put it all in real estate and mining sites, and media, election infrastructure, and politicians. You name it, I'm in it! The profits surpassed the costs very fast, so this prank paid for itself in no time. But if you had just stayed away from The City of Clouds, from me, none of this would've happened to you. Your tragedies are all your fault."*

Crow glares at the projected audio box. Its waves flare and stagger as Jay's boastful laughter dies down to giggles, and eventually he catches his breath.

"Man, that was funny watching those bodies fly away. Pretty sure your girl is dead, but maybe not. Hard to say with the camera feed going out. But even if she isn't, she will be soon enough. Claymores are a bitch," says Jay.

"I'm going to kill you, and enjoy every second of it," says Crow.

"I'll be waiting, sport."

Jay's audio feed cuts out, and Crow stands up and looks at the pirates on the bridge.

"Lock and load. We're killing Jay Azure," says Crow.

Good Night, Little Bird

Robin stands off to the side, refusing to look at Ibis while Blackbird breaks open the Communication Cloud's medical box to confiscates rolls of bandages. He makes quick work of applying more disinfectant to Robin's hands and re wrapping them in fresh bandages. She doesn't look at Blackbird, either. She's not mad at him, but she doesn't feel like looking at anybody in general.

Ibis and Sparrow are by the door, watching the perimeter, and Jay hasn't said anything to them in a while. But the silence is broken when a crackle and pop come from the operating computer. At first, no one registers it since they are lost in their own worlds, but then a voice breaks through the noise.

"This is Rebecca Station oh–one–five. City of Clouds, *please respond!"* says a man over the radio.

The group looks at the one working computer, and when the message repeats, Blackbird rushes to the computer and grips the console tight while speaking into its radio.

"This is *City*, I hear you loud and clear," says Blackbird.

"We've been trying to reach you for hours! We lost contact with our ice ship and when we sent out a search party, we found its wreckage zipping through space and your habitat gone! Now we picked up your SOS and a lifeboat of civilians. Where are you? Is everything alright?" says the man on the other end.

"Um... no. *The City of Clouds* is occupied by pirates. We've been trying to fight them off, but they hijacked your ship and used it to slip through, they jammed our signals, and have killed a whole lot of people. We need help and fast."

"That's what the lifeboat said. We can't do much. We're just ice miners. But my

overseer is listening in, and he's already contacted the Andromeda System Fleet. Help is on the way. Just hang in there and we'll get you out."

"Thanks. We're not sure how many pirates are left, but every bit you can give will help. We're going to need a lot of medical supplies and body bags."

"Help is on the way. Just stay safe."

"Roger that. *City* out."

Blackbird shuts off the radio, grips the sides, and takes a deep, long breath. Robin hesitates and goes to him.

"So... are we going to be okay?" asks Robin.

Blackbird shakes his head. "I want to say yes, but the pirates are still on here. We won't be safe until they're gone, and there's no telling how long until help arrives."

"We can hold up here, or take a lifeboat," says Ibis.

"We must assume that Crow is still operating the cameras, so if he is, he'll know we're here. Our best bet is to keep moving. We might even have to take him out ourselves," says Blackbird.

"Actually, you need to get to the bridge, ASAP," says Jay over the speaker.

The group looks at the cameras nearest to them.

"Crow's sweetheart was blown up by my vault, so he's a little pissed-off right now, and he and his entourage are on their way to kill me," says Jay casually. *"But my security will handle him. You get to the bridge and secure it so we can get things back on track quickly. You do this, and I promise big rewards are coming for all of you."*

Blackbird looks at the group. Robin nods, Ibis gives a thumbs up, and Sparrow grins.

"I do love the idea of a reward," says Sparrow.

Blackbird looks at the camera. "Alright, we'll get to the bridge in no time."

"Glad to hear. I'll see you guys soon," says Jay.

The intercom clicks off, and Blackbird takes a deep breath and grips the computer tight while bowing his head and taking a deep, shaky breath. Robin goes to him and rubs his shoulder.

"Are you okay?" asks Robin.

"Yeah. I'm relieved that this is almost over, but I also don't want to relax until I see Crow dead," says Blackbird.

"Hey, don't worry about Crow. Let's worry about something more important," says Sparrow. "Like, how are you going to spend your reward money? I hope I get lots of money because I want a Bugatti Nebula Rider."

The group looks at him, all frowning.

"What?" asks Sparrow.

"You're thirty-five percent committed, remember? If anything, you deserve thirty-five percent of what Captain Jay is offering," says Blackbird.

"Yeah, I know the whole thirty-five percent thing seems crappy, but with my thirty-five percent commitment combined with your guys' one hundred percent, you more than compensate for what I don't want to do. We all win," says Sparrow.

The group keeps staring at him in silence, until it is broken by Robin's voice.

"Sparrow, you're too precious to be in our group," says Robin.

Sparrow smiles brightly. "Thank you."

Robin frowns, and Blackbird shakes his head and goes to the door. Ibis approaches Robin.

"Let's get out of here. We need to get to the bridge quickly," says Blackbird.

"Right behind you!" says Sparrow.

Sparrow follows Blackbird out. Ibis stops in front of Robin, blocking her from the door, and she glares at him.

"Can we talk?" asks Ibis.

"No," says Robin.

Then she pushes her way past him, and he sighs heavily and walks after her.

"Yeah, I deserve this," mutters Ibis.

The group walks in silence after exiting the Communications Cloud. Blackbird is in the lead, followed by Robin close behind him, then it is Sparrow, and lastly, Ibis. They're not exactly sure what kind of path they are taking, but they know that they must get to the bridge.

They pass through multiple doors, travel down the pathways, look at the cameras scattered throughout, and much to their surprise and worry, they have not come across any pirates. They have come across dead guards, but that is about it. However, as much as they want to ask the question, none of them do, because they all silently agree that they have no idea where the rest of the pirates are.

After passing through another pathway, they enter an area with a row of glass doors and a bombastic sign with holographic projections of animals and people swirling and dancing around it. The sign says, *"The City of Clouds Holo-Theater."*

They keep walking, but Sparrow stops and looks at it, shaking his head sadly.

"You know, the last time I was here, this place was shut down due to safety reasons. And now that I'm back, I am still unable to enjoy this place," says Sparrow.

Robin and Ibis stop to look at Sparrow and the holo-theater, and Blackbird takes a few more steps before he realizes what's happening. He sneers at the group, while Ibis goes to Sparrow's side.

"I remember. I was disappointed too, but they failed the safety inspection, so there was nothing they could do," says Ibis.

"Ten fedos says they just bribed the next safety inspector," says Sparrow.

"I can see that happening."

"Why do you even want to go there? These places are boring," says Robin.

Sparrow and Ibis swiftly look at Robin.

"Seriously?" says Sparrow.

"What holo-theaters did you go to?" asks Ibis.

"All of them. They all suck," says Robin.

"I'm calling bullshit," says Sparrow.

"Me too," says Ibis.

Blackbird shakes his head and goes to the group.

"We don't have time for this. We need to keep moving," says Blackbird.

"When this is over, I'm taking Chickadee shopping for real clothes and a trip to the holo-theater," says Sparrow.

Robin scrunches her brows, and Blackbird grabs her arm.

"No, I'm taking her on real dates. You're just a weirdo who got traumatized by a dirty bathroom," says Blackbird.

"Can we not do this?" says Robin.

"I'll have you know that what was in that bathroom was the equivalent of a moldy chocolate velvet cake smothered in nutty chocolate syrup detonated in a toilet with firecrackers," says Sparrow.

The group groans and talks over each other to vocalize their disgust, but Sparrow keeps going.

"There were hand prints streaking on the wall and the stall, and it was on the floor. It bled into the next stall!" says Sparrow. "So, tell me, how could I remain a woman, knowing that women are filthy animals of extreme fecal destruction?"

Ibis' face contorts with disgust, and Sparrow grabs Robin and holds her close to him.

"And how could I let Chickadee remain trapped in her flawed form and terrible fashion sense? I will save Chickadee from herself." Sparrow looks dramatically to the ceiling. "I'll save all of us from ourselves."

The group is silent for a few seconds, and then Blackbird frowns and pulls Robin away from Sparrow.

"We're moving. Now," says Blackbird.

"Hold on, what about the whole, used to be a woman part?" says Ibis.

"Don't care. We have a job to do," says Blackbird.

"Yeah, we have a job to do," says Sparrow.

Nobody says anything after that, and when they are halfway to the exit, the door nearest to their destination opens, and Oro steps out with his group of pirates flanking him. Both sides stop moving and stare at each other like deer in headlights.

Then everyone snaps up their weapons.

"There they are!" shouts Oro.

"Into the theater!" orders Blackbird.

Both sides shoot at each other, and Blackbird kills one of the pirates while Ibis shoots out the glass doors to *The City of Clouds Holo-Theater*. He turns and shoots at the pirates with Blackbird, providing suppressive fire while Robin and Sparrow duck inside. Ibis and Blackbird follow them in, and Oro's group gives chase.

The City of Clouds Holo-Theater is a spacious, circular area with multiple rooms blocked by fogged-glass doors. There's a ticket booth, a concession stand, and an arcade room off to the side. Holographic images start playing in front of everyone as soon as they step through the door, but they are ignored while the group scatters.

A pirate runs towards them and fires several rounds, narrowly missing Robin and Ibis. Robin shrieks and stumbles, and Ibis shoves her to cover behind a half-wall and shoots at the pirate, striking him in the vest.

The pirate drops to the floor, but before Ibis can finish him, more bullets narrowly miss him, shattering displays and breaking holographic projectors, causing various images to break apart into pixels.

Ibis scrambles to cover behind some chairs, and he peeks out and sees Oro moving in.

"Kill them all!" yells Oro.

Pirates run past him, sweeping the area. Then one of the pirates stops suddenly when he sees Ibis, and he pulls a grenade off his vest and throws it at Ibis.

Ibis swears and runs, cursing up a storm as the other pirates shoot at him. The grenade detonates, the explosion roars loudly, and blasts Ibis through the fogged door of the arcade, scattering broken glass as he rolls across the floor.

"Ibis!" cries Robin.

The pirates shoot at her, and she ducks. Bullets hit a display case right above her head, raining shards down on her. She screams and covers her face with her hands, shaking violently.

When the dust settles, Ibis stands back up, covered in blood, and he quickly shoots two pirates dead, one being the pirate that threw the grenade at him.

Oro then shoots at Ibis, forcing him deeper into the arcade. The beastly man growls and keeps shooting as he closes in on Ibis.

Nearby, Blackbird kills three pirates with a wild spray of gunfire. And as the battle rages between the group and the pirates, a loud screech echoes throughout the Holo-Theater, and a giant black bird with fiery eyes and storm clouds descends from the sky, its wings spread wide.

"BIRD!" screams a pirate.

He shoots at the bird, and the avian and the clouds surrounding it fizzle out and completely disappears as projector pieces and sparks fall.

"Really, dumb ass? It was a projection!" says another pirate.

Those two pirates are swiftly shot dead by Blackbird, and he ducks around a corner as more pirates shoot at him. Blackbird takes potshots from his cover, and while doing this, he sees Oro going into the arcade. He curses and looks at Robin.

"Robin, cover me! I'm going to get Ibis!" says Blackbird.

Robin gulps and nods, and when Blackbird runs out of cover Robin shoots at the pirates, missing by a lot and popping more projections, causing animals, bugs, and scenery to break apart. The pirates snap at her and unload in her direction, forcing her to the floor.

Robin crawls on the floor as bullets rip through the half-wall, with large chunks collapsing and posters and photos behind glass displays being shredded. When she stops crawling, she lifts the rifle over her head and screams wildly as she she blindly shoots. The position is awkward, and the recoil from the weapon sends painful shocks through her hands, arms, and shoulders, but she keeps firing.

The pirates swear and scatter, and holographic projections flicker out, sparks and glass fly, and there are metallic snaps and groans. Then there is a louder snap, and a brief scream silenced by a loud thud and an explosion of sparks.

Robin keeps pulling the trigger until she hears clicks. Then she pulls the rifle down to her and shakily ejects her magazine and fumbles with the new one. After it is inserted, she takes deep, raspy breaths and pokes her head out of her cover.

She immediately cringes upon seeing a pair of feet sticking out from underneath the "Welcome" sign, which is now a mangled mess. Hanging from the ceiling are snapped cords and sparking wires.

"Die, bitch!" shouts a pirate.

Robin turns to the voice just in time to see bullets rip through his chest. He drops, and Sparrow walks up to her and holds out his hand.

"I've saved your life twice. When will you save mine?" teases Sparrow.

"You didn't save it twice," says Robin.

"Yeah, I did. Do you realize how much bacteria and possible infections I purged by dousing your hands in that bubbly stuff?"

Robin thinks for a moment. "Fair enough."

Then a weapon drops in front of them, and they stare at it for a moment before looking at where it came from. It is a pirate, holding his hands up.

"I surrender. You guys can have it. I'm done with this place," says the pirate.

Sparrow raises his brow. "Really?"

"Yep."

"Ah, well that's mighty nice of you. Have a good day, sir."

"You, too."

The pirate walks away after that, and Robin watches him go, but then Sparrow shoots him in the back until he drops. Robin looks at him, horrified.

"Why did you do that!?" yells Robin.

"Because he was a scumbag, and scumbags don't deserve to live. Now, where's Barfolomew and Aladdin?" says Sparrow.

As soon as he finishes his sentence, Blackbird flies out of the arcade and rolls across the floor. He stumbles, and dives out of the way from an arcade motorcycle flying towards him.

It bounces across the floor and smashes into a popcorn condiment stand. Then Oro rushes out with two pistols and shoots at Blackbird.

Blackbird swears and zigzags across the lobby and slides to cover behind the destroyed sign, which is where Robin is now hiding.

"Did he just throw that?" asks Robin in disbelief.

Blackbird is panting heavily. "Yeah. That guy's a freak."

"Time to be a hero," says Sparrow, who is hiding behind the ticket booth.

"Sparrow, no!" says Blackbird.

Sparrow jumps up with his rifle raised. "Die, pirate! OH SHIT!"

Sparrow ducks and a barrage of bullets strike the ticket booth and force Sparrow to lay on the floor. Robin pokes her head out and sees Oro stomping towards them and reloading. She shoots him in the chest, but all it does is make him flinch and growl, and he aims his pistols at her.

Robin ducks, and the bullets ricochet off the destroyed sign. She looks at Blackbird with wide eyes, and he nods knowingly.

"Told you," says Blackbird.

"The guy's a maniac!" says Sparrow from his cover.

"Hey!" yells Ibis.

Oro, Robin, Sparrow, and Blackbird look out and see Ibis storming out of the arcade, wielding a high-striker mallet.

Oro tilts his head, and Ibis screams and swings it against Oro's side. Oro stumbles and grunts, and Ibis whacks him again, knocking him on his back.

Oro quickly rolls to avoid another whack, and when he aims his pistols at Ibis, they are knocked out of his hand. Then Oro is whacked off his feet again.

Robin, Blackbird, and Sparrow cheer.

"Yeah, kick his ass, Aladdin!" shouts Sparrow.

Ibis hits Oro again, and when he goes for another hit, Oro grabs the mallet with one hand, stopping it cold. Then he growls and stands up, grabs it with his other hand, and snaps its handle into pieces. Ibis' eyes bulge and his colors drain from his face.

"Shit," says Ibis.

Robin and Blackbird leap to their feet and shoot at Oro, but the bullets only tear his skin or damage his vest, but nothing else. He kicks Ibis away, and stomps towards Blackbird and Robin. He punches Blackbird to the floor, and grabs Robin and slams her into the wall of photos. Glass shatters, and Robin gasps in pain. Then he throws her to the floor and stomps on her gut.

Robin jerks and curls on the floor, coughing and wheezing, and when Oro lifts his foot for a stomp on her head, Ibis stabs him in the side with the broken mallet handle. Oro grunts and stumbles, and then he grabs Ibis, yanks out his knife, and stabs Ibis in the shoulder.

They both scream as Oro barrels forward, forcing Ibis backwards towards a nearby holo-theater room. The glass door shatters against Ibis' back, and the two crash to the floor. Shards of glass scatter, and they roll to their feet. Ibis yanks the knife out with a pained grunt, and glares at Oro.

Oro growls, rips off a piece of holographic machinery from the wall, making the swarm of butterflies disappear, and he throws it at Ibis.

Ibis dodges it, and Oro rushes him. Ibis tries stabbing him, but Oro grabs his hand, twists the knife out with a loud crunch, and punches Ibis in the nose. The cartilage breaks, splashing his face with blood.

While Ibis stumbles back, Oro kicks him into the wall, breaking more holographic orbs, leading to the wall of vines fizzling out and pixelated or faded vines hanging around in uneven patterns. Sparks fly from the broken orbs, and Ibis falls to his knees with his back burnt.

Blood drips from his face to the floor as he breathes heavily, while Oro picks up his knife. Ibis growls painfully, grabs a shard of glass, and rushes Oro.

Oro and Ibis both scream, and Oro swipes at Ibis, but he slides out of the way and slashes Oro's arm. Oro whirls to try another strike, but Ibis avoids him once again and slices him. This goes on for a few more cycles, with Oro getting more cuts on his arms and legs, and Ibis's hand dripping blood from the glass digging into him.

Oros rushes Ibis again, and Ibis plunges the shard into Oro's kidney, however, Oro's speed is too much, and he rams Ibis into another projection pillar, snapping it into pieces and showering the two with sparks while causing the projected flora to flicker out of existence.

The pair roll on the floor, with Ibis coughing and Oro growling. Ibis holds his gut and feels hot blood oozing all over his hand. He gets on his knees and sees Oro's knife in him. His heart races, and his eyes widen. Oro kneels in front of Ibis, grabs him by the back of his head, and pushes the knife further in.

Ibis grunts and blood trickles out of his mouth while Oro smiles at him.

"*Buenas noches, pajarito,*" says Oro.

"Ibis!" shouts Blackbird.

Bullets suddenly hit Oro in the back, causing him to fall on top of Ibis. Sparks fly from Oro as the bullets expose cybernetic parts. Oro snaps around, snarling at Blackbird, and Blackbird's eyes narrow.

"Why won't you die already, you freak!" says Blackbird.

Oro runs after Blackbird, and Blackbird backs up while shooting at him. The bullets strike the cyborg and send out more sparks and blood as his flesh and cybernetic parts are damaged. When Oro reaches Blackbird, he punches him in the gut, sending him sliding across the floor with the air knocked out of him. As this happens, Robin crawls to her hands and knees, coughing and holding her gut.

"Blackbird," wheezes Robin.

She grabs her rifle and tries shooting Oro, but her rifle clicks, and Oro looks at her. His eyes narrow, hers widen, and he approaches her. Robin shrieks and backs up, while wielding her empty weapon like a club.

She hits him with it. He blocks it with his arm, and then he whacks it away, grabs Robin by the throat and lifts her off the ground.

Robin gags and claws at his wrist and hand, and he glares at her for a moment before he sees the jagged piece of metal covering one of his pirates. Oro smirks, drags Robin to the death pile, and her screams are weak and wheezy. Her heart races, her lungs burn, her vision gets hazy, and her feet kick the ground.

Then a bullet hits Oro in the head, blowing off a piece of his cheek and jaw. He drops Robin, and as she gasps for air, Oro holds his face, cursing up a storm. Blood gushes from his wound, and when he looks at who shot him, he sees Sparrow with a rifle.

Sparrow smirks and walks closer. "Only I'm allowed to mess with Chickadee."

Robin scrambles behind Sparrow, and Blackbird rolls on his hands and knees, coughing and wheezing. Meanwhile, Sparrow keeps walking and shoots at Oro, who goes behind the cover of the concession counter.

The soda machine is destroyed, spraying the area with sticky syrup, the candy is shot to pieces, and stale popcorn spills out while Sparrow unloads on the area, laughing maniacally.

"Oh yeah! Feel my wrath, pirate scum!" shouts Sparrow as holographic projectors make various colorful birds and animals fly and skip around from numerous positions.

Blackbird grabs his rifle and rushes to the counter. He leans over, then reels back when a bullet nearly blows his head apart.

"He's still got ammo!" shouts Blackbird.

Sparrow keeps shooting until his rifle clicks, and by that time, the concession stand is a mess of shattered glass, soda syrup, popcorn, and broken candy. Sparrow slings his rifle, draws his pistol, and carefully approaches the counter with Blackbird.

Robin scampers to a dead pirate, takes their rifle, and joins the other two. When they are in position, Blackbird nods, and all three shoot at the counter, reducing it to broken glass and metal splinters.

They remain still after that, with smoke rising from their barrels and their ears ringing. However, a few seconds later, Oro jumps up, bloodied with flaps of skin and muscle hanging from robotic enhancements, and his body covered in blood and other fluids.

He shoots Blackbird in the vest, dropping him. He snaps toward Robin and Sparrow, also shooting at them.

They scramble for cover, and Blackbird curses and rolls to his feet. He reaches for a fresh magazine and loads it right as Oro leaps to him.

Blackbird aims, Oro punches him in the face, and while his vision swims and blood gushes from his broken nose, Oro presses his pistol into Blackbird's throat and pulls the trigger.

Click.

Oro grunts and Blackbird sighs with relief, and small doves fly around them via holographic projection. Blackbird takes the moment of confusion to break Oro's grip on him and then rams him into a display of bottled drinks.

The display door shatters, the shelves break, and bottles roll on the floor. Oro kicks Blackbird away, and then he picks him up and throws him into a holographic pillar, breaking it into pieces and causing the birds to disappear.

While Blackbird tries to get up, Oro kneels on top of him, grabs a piece of the broken projector, and brings it down on him.

Blackbird grabs Oro's wrists and yells through gritted teeth as his arms burn to keep the sharp metal from piecing him. Oro's blood and robotic fluids drip on Blackbird, and he snarls and grabs Blackbird's throat.

Blackbird gags and kicks, and his arms struggle more to hold back the crude weapon. A grin creeps on Oro's torn-up face, and Blackbird's heart races as the jagged tip gets closer to his chest.

Nearby, a holographic projection on the floor shows overlapping images of flowers swirling in the wind and fish swimming in the sea. The pictures clash and pixelate, and then Robin swings her rifle stock against Oro's head. There is a loud crack, and Oro's head snaps to the side and breaks through the holographic projector's orb.

The jagged glass pierces his neck, and his body jerks and spasms as electric currents surge through him, sparking out and arcing through his burnt head. Then the projector explodes, sending bits of bone, brain matter and metal flying.

The metal strikes the last pirate in the gut as he snuck up on the group. Robin and Blackbird turn around and look at the pirate while he gags and drops his shotgun to clutch his pouring wound. Then he falls face-first on the floor, hitting his forehead on the broken concession stand, breaking his skull open.

Robin gasps and holds her hand over her mouth, Blackbird stares at the mess with wide eyes, and the dead pirate twitches as his blood seeps across the floor. Then there is Sparrow. He is grinning from ear to ear and wiping himself off.

"Oh... Oh man," says Blackbird.

"That was cool," says Sparrow.

"No! That's... That's not cool! Those are bad ways to go!" cries Robin.

She points at Oro A. Guila. His headless corpse is slowly burning from the inside out by the electric fire and filling the air with the stench of burnt flesh and electronics.

"He doesn't have a head anymore!"

Robin points at the other pirate, whose broken skull is poking through his skin.

"He's just dead! And he..."

Robin points to the pirate crushed under the broken sign.

"He's squished!"

Blackbird and Sparrow look at each other, and Robin grabs her hair and screams as she paces in circles.

"Why can't they die normally around me? Like get shot and just die?" cries

Robin.

"Maybe because they suck?" offers Sparrow.

"Shut up, Sparrow," snaps Robin. "And where's Ibis?"

Blackbird and Sparrow look around, and so does Robin. They don't see him anywhere in the carnage. Every now and then, a broken holographic projection of a person or animal will flicker into view before breaking apart into pixels.

"Ibis?" calls Robin.

"Hey, Ibis, where are you?" yells Blackbird.

"Hotel thief, where'd you go!" hollers Sparrow.

Robin goes to Blackbird and grabs his arm. She looks at him, her eyes wide and wet with panic, and his eyes weighted with concern.

"Where did you see him last?" asks Robin.

"I..." Blackbird stops himself and looks over his shoulder, and the others look at the shattered glass door. "Ibis!"

Blackbird bolts to the broken doorway, and Robin follows close behind, while Sparrow keeps his distance. The group enters the room and sees a streak of blood on the floor leading to the wall.

A pixelated safari man appears with large plants and bugs, but he and the scenery flicker out while the ambiance warbles, fuzzes, and pops in and out. The dim lights pulse, and Robin and Blackbird follow the blood until they see Ibis slumped against the wall, soaked in blood, holding his gut with a knife in deep. His eyes are closed, and his head is slumped forward.

"Ibis!" cries Robin.

Robin runs to Ibis and slides in next to him, clutching his hand. His hand is cold and weak, and his breathing is labored.

"Ibis? Ibis, can you hear me!" says Robin frantically.

She pats his face and rubs his hand, and Blackbird stops behind her, while Sparrow remains in the doorway.

"Ibis, please open your eyes," says Robin.

She pats his face again while tears soak her cheeks. Ibis takes a strained, wet, wheezy breath and opens his eyes to look at Robin. They are glazed and have trouble focusing.

"Robin?" says Ibis, his voice scratchy and weak.

Robin nods and smiles, blinking tears out of her eyes and rubbing his face.

"It's okay. I'm here," says Robin.

"I'm sorry," says Ibis. "I really am... That's all I wanted to say... Back there. I'm sorry."

Robin's lips quiver, and she whimpers and squeezes his hand tight, while tears roll down her bloody face. She gasps for air and rubs his hand, and Blackbird looks down.

"I forgive you," says Robin.

Ibis's lips twitch, and tears roll from his dim wet eyes as he puts his other hand on top of hers.

"Thank you," wheezes Ibis.

Then his eyes close, his hand slides off Robin, and his breathing stops.

"Ibis?" says Robin.

Ibis remains still, and Robin shakes his shoulder.

"Ibis?" repeats Robin, her voice cracking.

Ibis' blood touches Robin's pants. He remains silent and limp, and Robin's kneeling position breaks as she falls on the floor, her eyes wide and wet and her breathing hitched. She quietly stares at Ibis, too shocked to speak. Blackbird goes behind her and drapes his lucky jacket on her, before helping her stand.

"Come on," says Blackbird, hugging her and gently pulling her away.

Robin reluctantly grabs Blackbird's hand but doesn't look away from Ibis as they leave the destroyed area.

When they leave the room, Sparrow stands in the doorway, staring at Ibis' corpse. He flashes him a quick smile and walks after the others.

Punishment

Crow squeezes the stress ball in his hand as he marches down the hallway with his pirates. He has fifteen remaining, and Oro has a few as well.

Speaking of Oro...

Crow activates his communicator and selects his first mate.

"Oro, where are you?" said Crow.

Silence.

"Oro?"

More silence, and Crow's hand pumps the tattered stress ball as his teeth grind.

"Oro, are you there!?"

The pirates pass through a doorway and march down the connecting tube towards a stairwell. When there is no response from Oro, Crow growls, opens the door to the stairwell, and stomps up the stairs.

"Asshole's probably dead like everyone else," says Crow.

Their steps increase in speed, and when they get to their desired level, they file out of the stairwell, each readying their weapons while Crow glares ahead.

*****

In the captain's suite, Jay Azure watches Crow and his pirates travel quickly down the hallway while he writes names down on five hundred fedo-valued *Klumsy K's* gift cards for Blackbird's group. He wipes his face and paces nervously, while his guards move furniture around to make a barricade.

Jay's heart races, his hands tremble, and he plucks a liquor bottle off the floor. He takes a big gulp of alcohol before grabbing a pistol. While this happens, one of his guards approaches him and ushers him to the back of the suite.

"Sir, stay behind us," says the guard.

"Yeah, yeah, I got it," says Jay. After he is put in the back, he takes a deep breath and paces in circles while tapping his pistol against his thigh. "I'm going to retire after this... Yep, retire and play bingo for the rest of my life."

"You and me both," says a guard near him with a nervous smile.

Jay glares at him. "Fuck off. You're paid to do this. Not me."

The guard's smile drops, and he sulks away. Jay exhales and looks at a dead fish on the floor, covered in colorful pebbles and shards of glass.

"I'm definitely retiring after this."

*****

Somewhere in *The City of Clouds*, Nightingale stumbles out of a stairwell and flops to the floor, covered in blood, torn clothes, and poorly crafted bandages made from the clothes of her fallen pirates. She pushes herself to her feet and clutches her arm as she limps down the hallway. She uses her injured hand to try to turn on her communicator, but all she gets is fuzz and error messages.

"Come on, come on, come on," mutters Nightingale.

She passes through a doorway, and it seals behind her.

Some seconds later, another doorway opens, and Raven comes out with her backpack considerably lighter, and she is also messing with her communicator.

"Sparrow? Ibis? Anybody hear me?" asks Raven.

No reply.

Raven stops for a moment and groans to the ceiling; when she is done with that, she goes to a pillar displaying a map and studies it.

"Of course, they don't answer," says Raven. "Do they even have a communicator? I don't even know why I took this job. This job is dumb!"

She taps the map and hurries off in the direction she needs to go.

"I'll get the money and disappear for good! That is a good plan. You got this Raven. You totally got this!"

*****

Crow leads his pirates down the pathway, breathing heavily and glaring at the only door at the far end. As they walk, one of the pirates pulls out explosive bricks from his backpack.

They reach the suite's door, and the pirate sticks the bricks in the corners and center of the door. The bricks are primed, the pirates press themselves on the hallway wall, and Crow nods.

"Blow it."

*****

Inside the suite, Jay and his guards stare at the door. Sweat scratches at their skin, their clammy fingers shift on their rifles. They hear multiple thuds on the door, and they adjust their positions.

"Steady... Steady..." orders one of the guards.

There is silence for a few seconds, and then there are five overlapping explosions that send metal bits flying into the room with colorful smoke rolling in. The pirates rush in, screaming and shooting wildly. Their bullets quickly reduce the barricades to splinters, and the guards shoot back while shouting orders or insults.

Jay scrambles around as the bullets strike the areas near him. Guards and pirates drop as they exchange gunfire, and some get close for hand-to-hand combat, either punching or using their knives to slash and stab.

Some bullets strike the windows, leaving chips in it, and Jay curses and runs to the bar, keeping his head down when pirates try shooting him.

"No, he's mine!" shouts Crow, before shooting a guard through the head.

"Someone, kill that maniac!" yells Jay, while aiming his pistol at Crow.

He shoots at Crow, and Crow runs across the suite, shooting back. Bullets from Crow shatter bottles and splash Jay with alcohol and glass and force him to cover with thin trails of blood on his face from glass nicking him. Bullets from Jay strike Crow in the vest and graze his bicep, knocking him down.

Crow quickly rolls to the kneeling position and guns down another guard, and then dives behind a couch and lays low. Bullets tear apart everything around him as a few of Jay's guards focus on him.

The couch guts fly, his pirates drop one by one, the elegant bar and its expensive contents are reduced to splinters and shards of glass. The thunder and rattles of gunfire clashing with the screams and shouts is music to his ears, but every concert needs to end.

Crow peeks out of cover, just to retreat when a barrage of bullets strikes near him, nicking him with ricochet. But at that moment of inspection, he sees what he needs to do.

"Birdies, hold on tight!" orders Crow.

Crow switches out his pistol, readies his rifle, and aims at the window.

"Oh shit," says a pirate.

Jay peeks out and sees where Crow is aiming.

"Don't you dare, you maniac!" shouts Jay.

Jay shoots at Crow, knocking him down again. While lying on the floor, Crow shoots at the window separating the suite from the void. Little nicks in the glass grow to cracks, and the cracks spread to make spider web patterns.

After that, the glass breaks under his onslaught of bullets, and a deafening howl with a rush of wind sucking everyone and everything towards the hole leaves Crow momentarily discombobulated. However, he recovers and grabs the railing before space claims him.

This cannot be said for his stress ball, or Jay's guards and some of the pirates, plus the corpses and Jay's broken possessions. The chandelier lights pop, and its broken bulbs, plus dead fish, broken glass, wooden shards, bullet casings and weapons are sucked into the cold expanse of space, where they tumble out of sight.

Almost as quick as it begins, it ends with multiple thuds from metal sleeves slamming down over the windows.

Emergency lights swirl and air is pumped back into the room. Crow hears his remaining pirates and Jay coughing and cursing over the alarm and automated calls to evacuate.

Crow stands up and groans loudly, and then he rolls his neck and shoulders. His eyes and teeth gleam in the falling sparks and red swirling emergency lights.

"I am not doing that again," laughs Crow.

He draws his knife and twirls it as he walks around the barren room, searching for his target. His remaining pirates are slowly getting back up. Some stagger, and others are heaving and coughing. He sees five pirates remaining, and that makes his blood boil.

It was hard enough recruiting pirates, and it was hard enough finding worthy replacements after raids when one or two inevitably die from ship security. But now he has been reduced to five pirates on this raid, all thanks to this stupid habitat.

Crow shakes his head and sighs heavily. Then he sees a body briefly appear in the swirling red lights. He a wolfish grins spreads as he twirls his knife again.

"Captain Jay Azure!" calls Crow, his voice booming in the hollowed suite.

Jay growls and pulls himself up, using the fractured remains of the bar for support.

"You're a lunatic, you know that?" says Jay.

Crow hurries his steps, and Jay glares at him.

"You may kill me now, but I have connections. They will hunt you down and kill you, your family, your pirates, and their families! They'll even kill your parrots!" yells Jay.

Crow grabs Jay and plunges the knife into his gut. Jay gasps, and Crow grabs the back of Jay's head and speaks in his ear.

"Joke's on you, Captain. I don't own a parrot," says Crow.

Then he rips the knife out at an angle and stabs Jay again, and he keeps doing this repeatedly. Each stab brings out a pained grunt and a wet gurgle from Jay.

Jay drops to his knees, and Crow holds his hair as he slashes his throat. By the time Crow is done, Jay's torso is fleshy ribbons, his throat is flaps, and his blood covers both bodies.

Crow throws Jay's mangled corpse to the floor and turns to his pirates. They stare at him quietly, and he wipes his face with his bloody hands, and then his knife on his vest.

"Let's get out of here," says Crow.

"But what about the money?" asks a pirate.

"There is no money! We've been played! And when I find our employer, I'm going to kill him slowly, but we need to get off this ship first. So, gather yourselves and get to the lifeboats."

The pirates nod and go to the door, but halfway there, Crow's communicator activates, and a broken holographic projection of an audio box appears.

"Crow... Crow... can you hear me?" says Nightingale.

Crow stops and orders his pirates to do the same. They comply and look at him, and he turns on his end of the communicator with a shaky hand and racing heart.

"Love? Nightingale is that you?" says Crow swiftly, his lips twitching to a smile.

"Finally! Yes, it's me... I'm injured, but I am heading to the bridge. The vault was rigged! It killed everyone but me, but it got me good," says Nightingale.

"I'm not on the bridge anymore. But I just killed the captain in his suite, so when you get to the bridge, stay there, and wait for me. I'll get you out of here."

"How many of us are left?"

"I haven't been able to contact Oro, so I am going to say it is you, me, and the five with me."

"Good grief... Fuck this ship. Seriously, fuck it to death."

Crow chuckles. "Couldn't agree more, Love. Hang tight. I'm on my way."

Crow hangs up and looks at his pirates.

"Change of plans. We're going back to the bridge."

One Less Bird

Raven's body ached as she runs down the corridor of *The City of Clouds*. It takes all of her remaining energy just to keep moving forward. But she has no choice. She must keep going. She must get to the bridge quickly.

She may have done something insane for a hefty paycheck, but she won't let anymore people die. Enough blood has been spilled today and she'll be damned if more people die because of her job.

Right now, Raven is the only one who can help whoever is left on the habitat. And besides, saving the remaining people is the least she can do, especially after planting the bombs around the Engine Cloud.

And so Raven presses onward toward the habitat's central hub. As she runs, she wonders why the hell she agreed to do the job, anyway. Sure, the money was excellent, enough to retire and disappear even, but she should've refused this job outright. Now she has a chance to absolve some of her sins by saving the lives of others. Maybe she needs to take another look at what kind of life she wants to lead once she retires.

Maybe build a wildlife refuge? Or work in a soup kitchen? Maybe build an orphanage? Donate to the Unity church? The Catholic Church? Any church of any denomination? Convert to Buddhism?

God and gods alike know with the amount of money heading her way she'll be able to do just about anything. Not that Raven cares much anymore. All she really wants is a clean conscience. And saving the trapped passengers will deliver that. In fact, it might even redeem her soul entirely.

Raven has never stepped foot in a church or temple, but she is certain helping those less fortunate than ones self is what Unity teaches. And the six million denominations of Christians agree that Jesus Christ himself helped mankind during his time here on Earth. So if she saves the passengers and helps people with the loads of money that means she can get it into heaven, right? Or maybe she can use the money to build a fancy church or temple and donate it to which ever religious group is closer. The deities like the fancy stuff, and that can give her afterlife brownie points, too.

Raven smiles to herself and runs faster. Now that she thinks about it, it seems lots of money is just what she needs to wash away her bad choices, after all.

When Raven reaches the Commons Cloud, she stumbles to a pillar and takes a moment to catch her breath. Her lungs burn, her throat feels like nails are scraping it, and her legs are heavy and quivering. She swallows her spit to soothe her dry throat, and hobbles through the area, passing Bellona's statue and many corpses and trash that have been piled on top of each other in bloody heaps against the wall.

Bellona's red-tinted light shines down on the carnage through the massive glass dome above, and streaks of lightning surge through its gas bands.

Raven goes to the stairs and grips the rail tight as she climbs them to the next level. When she reaches the second floor, she sees the door to the bridge has been blown open. She swallows again, draws her pistol, and cautiously approaches the doorway, being sure to stay close to the wall.

As she walks, she listens for any signs of the pirates, but so far nothing. When she reaches the gaping hole leading to the bridge, she takes a deep, shaky breath, and peeks in. Much to her surprise and relief, the bridge is empty. There is some blood and corpses strewn about, and some of the computers are damaged, but no sign of the pirates. Raven lets out a sigh and goes inside, but she keeps her weapon drawn and her finger rests on the trigger guard.

"Hello?" calls Raven. "Is anyone alive in here?"

No response.

Raven slowly moves across the bridge, careful not to step on the bodies. She scans the area until she spots the captain's chair. It is empty, but all of the computers are on, and a physical manual is open.

Raven grabs the manual, and starts flipping through it, searching for the alarms section. It doesn't take long for her to find what she needs.

The alarms are:

Code 1 = Ship is entering high speed

Code 2 = Ship detected

Code 3 = Unknown ship detected

Code 4 = Pirate vessel detected

Code 5 = Alien spacecraft detected

Code 6 = Engine failure

Code 7 = System(s) failure (emergency meeting. Next COA TBD based on severity)

Code 8 = Atmospheric leak (evacuate area of effect)

Code 9 = Fluid leak (evacuate area of effect)

Code 10 = Bomb detected (mandatory evacuation)

She quickly reads through the manual to figure out how to turn on the Code 10 alarm. But while she does this, she doesn't notice someone walking across the bridge, covered in blood, torn clothes, and unsanitary bandages made from ripped shirts. The newcomer's hand grips her pistol tightly, and she is breathing heavily and glaring at Raven.

"You're not Crow," says Nightingale.

Raven jumps in her seat and looks up. Then her eyes widen when she sees Nightingale, and her face pales when Nightingale raises her pistol.

"You're not Crow," repeats Nightingale. She approaches Raven with wobbly steps and cocks her pistol. "Who are you, and where's Crow?"

"Lady, I've never seen Crow. I don't even know who you are!" says Raven.

"Liar! Crow said he'd be here, but he's not here! Where is he!"

"How should I know!?"

Nightingale continues forward and her pistol shakes in her hand while blood drips from her body, leaving dots on the floor.

"You know where he is. I know you do. Everyone else in my crew is dead, but you look a-okay! Are you with security? Are you with Officer Impostor? Who do you work for!?"

Raven shakes her head, then glances at the pistol on the desk.

"Look, calm down. Lower your weapon, and we can talk this out and get off this ship together," says Raven. "Nobody else has to die today."

"You killed Crow, didn't you?" accuses Nightingale.

"What are you talking about!? Just knock it off already! I don't know you or Crow! I don't know what the hell is going on with him or you, but I do know that we need to get out of this habitat right now. So, chill out, lower your weapon, and come with me so we can live another day, alright?"

"You killed him. That's why he's not here. You killed him!"

Raven's hand slides next to her pistol. "Lady, don't do this."

"You killed Crow, you mayo monkey fuck!"

Nightingale shoots at Raven, forcing her to duck. The bullets strike the computers, sending sparks flying, and Raven awkwardly initiates the Code 10 alarm, leading to a siren blaring throughout the entire habitat.

"Attention! This is a Code 10 evacuation! Bring only your IDs and report to the nearest lifeboat in an orderly fashion!" says an automated male voice.

The alarms continue ringing, and the automated voice repeats in a loop, drowning out the sound of gunshots. Both women are shooting wildly now, their guns blazing, bullets piercing computers and ricocheting off the environment.

Raven scurries through the rows of computers, keeping herself crouched while Nightingale shoots like a maniac. They both keep moving, trying to flank each other while exchanging gunshots.

Raven presses herself against one of the desks and breathes heavily as she ejects her spent magazine and slips in a new one. Her heart races, and she grits her teeth. She peeks around the desk, and retreats when a bullet narrowly misses her head.

Raven peeks out again a few seconds later with her pistol ready, only to find that Nightingale has moved closer than expected.

Nightingale fires a second round. Raven retreats behind the desk, just in time for another shot to narrowly miss her.

"There's no running! I've got you trapped!" says Nightingale.

Raven bangs her pistol against her forehead, quietly spewing out a series of curses. Then she notices out of the corner of her eye a nearby can of *Extra Strength & Length Bug Killer Spray*. She looks at the floor and sees Nightingale's shadow creeping towards her while it is pulled to and fro by the swirling emergency lights.

Raven grabs the can, and when Nightingale rounds the desk, Raven sprays her face with a long, thick stream of bug spray.

Nightingale shrieks and blindly fires a shot, striking Raven. Raven curses, and flops around, clutching her wounded shoulder while the spicy scent of the spray makes her nose burn.

Nightingale keeps screaming and cursing as her eyes sizzle, and she fires her pistol wildly. Raven ducks behind a row of computers and presses her hand harder against her bleeding shoulder while the erratic gunshots blow out lights, hit chairs, and break monitors.

Nightingale stumbles around and hits a desk, and flops to the ground, shrieking and swearing. She fumbles with her belt, feeling around for a new magazine.

When Nightingale grabs a magazine and attempts to pull it out while blood pours from her ruptured eyes, Raven jumps up and shoots Nightingale until her magazine is empty. When Raven is done shooting, she is breathing heavily and looking at Nightingale's corpse with wide eyes and an open mouth.

Blood is pouring from the multiple holes in Nightingale's body. The corpse is still twitching and her eyes and the area around them have dissolved or bubbled, leaving bloody pools and destroyed skin.

Raven ejects her empty magazine and puts her last one in. Then she wipes her bloody hands on her suit.

She stares at the dead woman's face, which appears to be contorted into a grimace of agony. Raven is still trembling and having a hard time breathing. A part of her is expecting Nightingale to get back up. But all that happens is the woman's body stops twitching.

Raven hesitates, then grabs Nightingale's last magazine and she stashes it on her belt. Then she backs up, holding her hand to her mouth and fighting to break the wet lump in her throat. She gasps for air, and then hurries out of the bridge.

The Last of the Murder

Distant, stampeding feet and screams and shouts, all terrified and urgent, echo through the red lit halls of *The City of Clouds*. Blackbird leads Sparrow and Robin down the pathway, passing frightened civilians scrambling to escape as an automated male voice speaks through the intercoms, mixing with the grating alarms.

"Attention! This is a Code 10 evacuation! Bring only your IDs and report to the nearest lifeboat in an orderly fashion!" says the voice.

The automated voice loops, and if Robin wasn't in a clash of adrenaline and melancholy, then the chaotic noises would put her in a state of confusion, but as of now, she has one clear thought: Kill Crow.

A small voice in the back of her mind is trying to tell her that she hated Ibis for what he did, which is true. But she didn't hate him that much. And everything that has happened today is because of Crow. All the deaths and the horrible memories to linger are on him, and if he isn't stopped, then he'll do this again.

Robin grips her weapon tighter and the light of Bellona shines on her, Blackbird, and Sparrow. Lightning surges through the gaseous planet's bands, and the group's speed-walking turns to fast jogs down the pathway.

"Great. It wasn't enough to raid the habitat. Now they're going to blow it up!" says Blackbird. "If there's any pirates left, I'll make sure they don't make it off this habitat."

"You really have a hate boner for pirates," says Sparrow.

"Well, I didn't become an Oliver Twist for no reason," says Blackbird.

"Wait, your name is Oliver Twist?" says Sparrow.

"It's the name of a myth he likes," says Robin.

"Oh... Lame," says Sparrow.

That conversation ends, and the group's jogging evolves to running. They keep running until they reach the Commons Cloud. They skid to a stop, and Sparrow uses a pillar for support as he takes raspy breaths of air, and Robin is panting, but following Blackbird.

His speed has slowed to heavy steps, and the red light of the gas giant shines down on them as they walk through the area, passing broken furniture, shattered dishes, spilled food and drinks, and corpses.

"We need to get to the bridge," says Blackbird.

"But the bomb thing," wheezes Sparrow.

"Captain Jay said he'll meet us at the bridge."

"Yeah, I heard, but–" Sparrow waves his arm around at the swirling lights *"THE BOMB!"*

"Sparrow's right, we really need to go to a lifeboat," says Robin, looking at Blackbird with worry.

"You two are free to go, then. There's a lifeboat nearby. Every habitat is regulated to have lifeboats or pods stored in every sector. But I'm waiting for the captain," says Blackbird.

"Oh... Neat," says Sparrow. He looks off to the side and frowns. "But if we're going to get to those lifeboats, we're going to have to probably shoot a few more guys."

Robin and Blackbird look to where Sparrow is looking. They snap their weapons up while Sparrow backs up.

"Why, hello there!" calls Crow over the alarm.

Crow and his pirates step into the Commons Cloud. The pirates are also aiming their weapons at the group, and Crow's free hand twitches as though it is squeezing an invisible object. The pirate captain is grinning broadly, and his eyes are fiery as he approaches the group.

"Do my eyes deceive me, or do I finally get to meet Officer Impostor and his buddies face to face?" says Crow.

"Yes, it is us!" says Sparrow. "Officer Impostor, the valiant; Chickadee the thingy; and I, Sparrow, the gem of the Prospect Sector."

"Chickadee?" Crow looks at Robin, and he takes a moment of processing before pointing at her. "Chickadee... As in, Chickadee_0052 from Galaxy Love Quest?"

Robin tilts her head up, groaning loudly. "Are you kidding me!? Another one!"

"How many dating apps do you have?" asks Blackbird.

Robin rubs her face and growls irritably. "Too many. I'm deleting all of them when I get out of here."

Robin then pats her pocket. Her hand abruptly stops. She frowns and pats her pants harder from her thighs to her butt. Then she sighs heavily and glares at no one in particular.

"Never mind. My phone is gone," says Robin.

"It was bugging me that I knew you from somewhere," says Crow. "But now that I know where I know you from, I gotta say, I messaged you, but you never returned my message, which I was Black–Feathers, just a little FYI. I even put you in my favorites list, just in case my other girl died or got arrested or something."

Crow glances around while pulsing the fingers of his free hand with tighter motions.

"Where is Nightingale, anyway?" asks Crow.

One of the pirates shrugs, but that is all he gets.

"I didn't answer you because you aren't my type," says Robin sourly. "And it's because of you that a lot of people died!"

Crow looks at Robin with shock.

"Not your type? It's the tattoos, isn't it?" says Crow, pointing to the tattoos covering his cheeks.

Robin's eyes narrow, and Crow waves dismissively.

"Never mind. Don't care. I'm going to kill all of you just like I killed your captain because every single one of you has been a pain in my ass!" says Crow.

"We already wiped out your army, Crow. This is the end of the line for you. How do you want to do this? Bullet, blade, or bludgeon?" says Blackbird.

"Bludgeon. Beat him like the naughty boy he is!" says Sparrow.

Robin and Blackbird sneer at Sparrow, and Crow's pirates move in front of their captain, creating a meat-wall between him and Blackbird's group.

"Still wanting to be a hero, eh?" chuckles Crow. He looks at the desolation around him. "You've done a bang-up job. Congrats. Congrats. Congrats! **CONGRATS!**"

Crow finishes with a stomp and glares at Blackbird's group.

"You know, this was supposed to be just a simple raid, right? Board the ship, take the money, and skedaddle on outta here." Crow waves his arms. "None of this was supposed to happen!"

"Right. Now you're going to tell us that you didn't plant the bomb on the habitat," says Blackbird.

"I didn't. But I am glad someone did. This place sucks! And as punishment for making things harder than they had to be, I'm going to kill everyone here."

"Yeah? How're you going to do that? You got no more manpower," says Blackbird.

Crow grins. "Do I?"

Suddenly, there is a bright flash of light from the glass dome above them, and Robin's group shields their eyes as they look up. When the light disappears, they lower their arms and stare wide-eyed as a brown ship with sharp curved edges and skeletal birds painted on its hull glides over them.

On its side, in bloody letters, is "*Murder, He Wrote.*"

With the ship gliding overhead, Crow looks at Blackbird, Robin, and Sparrow, holding his grin. They look at the ship with shock from Blackbird, horror for Robin, and a twitching lip from Sparrow.

"Perfect timing. It looks like my cavalry has just arrived! And boy is this going to be fun for me!" says Crow theatrically. "The rest of you can get bent."

"Oh shit," says Blackbird.

"Yeah. 'Oh shit' is right," says Crow. He turns on his communicator and aims his pistol at the group. "*Murder, He Wrote*, this is your captain speaking."

"*This is* Murder. *Good to hear you, Captain*," says a pirate.

"There are lifeboats getting ready to leave *The City of Clouds*. Shoot all of them. No survivors," orders Crow.

"No!" cries Robin, snapping at Crow with wide, wet eyes.

"Roger that, captain," says the pirate.

Crow cackles. "While you're at it, send a boarding party to pick up me and my birdies. We'll be in the main big ball area. Better hurry. Some jackass planted a bomb and I have no idea how much time we have."

"Roger that, Captain Magnolia."

"Crow, you sick fuck!" yells Blackbird.

Cannons roll out from *Murder, He Wrote*. The ship turns, and its boosters nudge it away from *The City of Clouds*.

"Hey, don't get mad at me! All of this could have been avoided if you didn't try to play hero," says Crow. "This tragedy is all your fault."

Sparrow looks up and sees Raven creeping on the upper level with a pistol in hand. He smiles thinly, and Crow looks at Sparrow.

"What are you smiling about?" asks Crow.

"Nothing. I'm just amused that all of us had a bad day," replies Sparrow.

"Yeah, I'll give you that. But it'll be better when all of you die."

Then there is a bright flash of fiery light above them, and everyone, including Raven, looks up and sees pieces of *Murder, He Wrote* twirling into space. The pirate ship shifts its position and turns its cannons, and another missile strikes it, blowing out a large chunk of it and sending quick bursts of fire rolling into space.

Its light flickers, and it fires off a few shots before a beam rips through it from nose to tail, popping it. Fire bursts out, its lights flicker, and huge pieces roll and spin into the void. Some of the debris strikes the Commons Cloud's dome, cracking it, and Crow screams furiously while his remaining pirates stare in disbelief.

"No! Are you kidding me!? What the hell!?" screams Crow. **"FUCK!"**

Lifeboats speed by the dome, with some going over or under the debris field, and others brave the twisted metal. Moments later, a featureless sewing needle-shaped ship with a silver hull glides into view.

"What the heck?" says Robin.

"That's a Section 0 ship," says Blackbird. "They sent a ship from Nyx to help us!"

Blackbird then notices Raven getting into position on the upper level, and he grins at Crow.

"You're fucked, pal," says Blackbird.

Crow glares at Blackbird, and he growls. He holsters his pistol, and aims his rifle at Blackbird, bringing his five remaining pirates to spread their formation. This also causes Robin, Sparrow, and Blackbird to spread out and back up.

"No! You're fucked! All of you are fucked! I'm going to fuck all of you to death! Then I'm going to fuck your corpses until your ghosts die!" screams Crow.

Raven suddenly shoots Crow in the back of the vest, knocking him forward, and everyone scatters and shoots wildly.

During the barrage, Robin is hit in the vest and her left arm, and she falls to the floor, screaming in pain. Bullets whiz over her, ricocheting off the walls and pillars, and she scrambles to cover behind one of the support pillars and clutches her wound. Raven fires two shots as she moves positions, hitting Crow in the leg, and he collapses to the ground.

"Fucking hell!" screams Crow. He crawls to cover behind the Bellona statue and ducks further down when Blackbird shoots at him. "Somebody, get rid of that damn pigeon!"

One of the pirates quickly spots Raven and shoots at her, shattering the glass panels, but she dodges and keeps firing blindly.

"Shoot her, shoot her!" yells Crow.

His pirates continue shooting at Raven, who continues dodging and taking potshots at them. A bullet finally hits Raven in the vest, and she stumbles backwards, out of their line of fire.

Sparrow shoots wildly, striking one of the pirates and killing him instantly, but another pirate shoots Sparrow in the vest, dropping him. The pirate rushes to finish off Sparrow, but while he's running, Robin empties her magazine into him.

After the pirate drops dead, Robin runs to Sparrow and inspects him while Blackbird kills another pirate. This leaves two pirates. And while Robin inspects Sparrow, Sparrow grabs her wrist and smiles at her with a lot of strain.

"Thanks for the checkup, but this changes nothing," says Sparrow.

"Sure it does. I owe you one less thing now," says Robin with an uneasy smile.

Blackbird goes out of cover and shoots at another pirate. The pirate scrambles to cover and blindly chucks a grenade at Blackbird. It rolls at his feet, and he kicks it away.

It bounces off a pirate's head, disorienting him for a moment. It lands near Robin. She and Sparrow yell, and Robin whacks it away with her rifle. It sails through the air and lands near Crow.Crow curses and kicks it away, leading it to roll underneath the Bellona statue base. Then it detonates, blowing off a corner.

The statue groans, and more of the damaged base snaps and pops, causing the statue to topple over and crash into the upper level, shattering more glass panes and bending the floor, while popping some lights and pipes.

The two remaining pirates seek cover, with one dragging Crow with him. They're trying to move towards the stairs, but when they reach the stairs, Raven unloads her magazine into one while Blackbird shoots the second one in the head, leaving just Crow.

Crow hobbles upright and paces in a circle, growling with aggravation while the group closes in on him. When they reach him, Crow sighs heavily and holds up his hands.

"Okay, okay, no need for violence," says Crow. "Let's talk this out."

He turns around slowly and looks at Robin, who has shouldered her weapon and is now clutching her wounded arm.

"Man, you're like a cockroach. I really would've loved you on my crew," says Crow. He looks at everybody. "In fact, all y'all have my respect. Never in all my years of pirating have I ever dealt with a group quite like you. Y'all want to make some money? I'm hiring. Good pay, lots of travel, and I have excellent dental coverage."

A gunshot rings out and Crow's head snaps back with blood splattering on the wall behind him. A second later, Crow falls sideways, lifeless.

The group stares at his corpse, stunned. Then they look at Blackbird, who is glaring at the corpse and gripping his smoking rifle tight.

The lights and noises of the alarm mean nothing now, and their eyes move away from Blackbird back to Crow's body. Then they silently stare at each other again, waiting for someone else to speak or do something.

But everyone keeps quiet, too shocked and exhausted by the events of the past few hours to think clearly anymore.

"That... was anticlimactic," says Sparrow.

Raven grips the handrail tight as she gingerly climbs down the stairs, and she stops by Sparrow's side.

"Can we *please* get off this ship, now?" asks Raven.

Blackbird nods and grabs Robin's hand.

"Yeah, let's get out of here. There should be more than enough lifeboats for us to use, considering what Crow did," says Blackbird.

Sparrow and Raven nod, and the group starts walking towards the exit. As they go, Robin looks at Crow's body. Sparrow smiles at her, and Raven hobbles next to him. Robin looks away and holds her wound tighter and continues moving forward, while leaning against Blackbird for support.

They make their way through the wrecked lobby, stepping carefully avoiding broken furniture, shattered glass and corpses. But right as they begin passing the toppled Bellona statue, a gunshot rings out, leaving Robin's ears ringing and her support suddenly disappearing.

Blackbird crumbles next to her with a hole in the back of his head, and Robin's eyes widen with shock. When she turns, Sparrow pistol whips her in the head, knocking her to the floor.

Robin's vision swims, and Sparrow kicks her weapon away before climbing on top of her and punching her repeatedly. Raven stays off to the side, cringing and looking away.

"You just! Had to! Be! A pain! In! The ass!" screams Sparrow with every punch. His face is red, and his veins are throbbing, and he gives one more punch, leaving Robin's face bruised and bloodied.

Robin gasps for air as blood soaks her mouth, neck, and her collar. Sparrow hoists her up by her collar and throws her against the Bellona statue base. Robin tumbles onto the ground, coughing blood, and she cries out in pain when Sparrow kicks her ribs.

Robin tries to crawl away from Sparrow, but he snarls and stomps on her back, sending sharp pains throughout Robin's abdomen. Robin groans in agony and curls herself into a ball, trying desperately to protect herself as Sparrow marches around her.

"Raven, get the cuffs from Blackbird," says Sparrow.

Raven keeps her eyes averted, and Sparrow glares at her.

"Raven! The cuffs!" yells Sparrow.

Raven hurries to Blackbird's corpse. Her hands tremble as she fumbles through his gear, and she nearly drops the cuffs when she retrieves them from his vest. Then she goes to Robin and cuffs her to a piece of the statue base.

"Sorry about this," says Raven.

Robin trembles, and she whimpers in pain. Her face is cracked, swollen, and bleeding, and her entire torso aches from the assault. Blood drips down her chin and onto the floor below her.

"I'm sorry," says Raven again, backing up and wiping tears from her eyes.

"Don't apologize to her," says Sparrow. "You had a job, and I had a mission, and we both accomplished it."

Sparrow wipes the blood off his knuckles, on Raven's jacket, and he aims his pistol at Robin.

"No..." whimpers Robin, staring up at Sparrow with her hand raised. "Please don't do this."

Sparrow thinks for a moment, and then he giggles and lowers his weapon.

"You're right. Killing you right here right now will be too easy for what you did to me. I will make your last moments hell for the torment you inflicted on me!" says Sparrow.

"Sparrow, we really need to go," says Raven.

"Are the bombs on a timer?" asks Sparrow.

"No. They're signal activated."

Sparrow scoffs. "Then stop worrying. We have time for the most magnificent monologue in this system's history!"

The Unforgivable Sin

Bellona's red light shines down on Robin, Sparrow, and Raven, and the sleek Section 0 ship remains positioned above *The City of Clouds*. The lights from the alarms and the gas giant reflect off the blood covering Robin's broken face.

Robin glares at Sparrow as he paces back and forth, waving his pistol around, saying something that Robin can't understand due to the mix of her ragged breathing, racing heart, and the habitat's alarm. But what she does catch is something about a monologue and a high school drama class.

"You bastard," says Robin weakly.

Sparrow looks at Robin. "What did you say?"

Robin spits out blood and a piece of tooth.

"You're a bastard," says Robin. "You were working for the pirates the whole time."

Sparrow chuckles and looks at Raven. His chuckle then turns to an obnoxious laugh that makes Raven step back, and Sparrow looks back at Robin.

"Another thing you ruined. I wanted to do a monologue, but you just had to be a heckler," says Sparrow. "And for the record, you are wrong, Chickadee. Wrong! I wasn't working for the pirates. They were working for me, thanks to a little ad I found on Dave's List. I hired them under the promise of them having everything in Jay Azure's vault. And you have no idea how much of a pain in the ass you and your friends were. You were supposed to just die tragically in a pirate attack, but *nooo~* you just had to be a bunch of menaces and ruin things!"

Sparrow sighs heavily and wipes the sweat off his bald head and stands next to Raven, while inserting a fresh magazine into his pistol.

"Whatever. I need to wrap this up. How many bombs are in the Engine Cloud?" asks Sparrow.

"There's more than enough explosives, because when the habitat sped up, it tore apart the pirate's ship, which means the bombs meant for them were put with the engines," says Raven.

Sparrow steps away from Raven, and Robin's heart races while Raven's worry grows.

"And they are signal activated, correct?" asks Sparrow.

Raven swallows and nods as she grips her pistol tighter.

"They are," says Raven after taking a breath.

"Awesome," says Sparrow.

Then he snaps at Raven as she brings up her pistol, and he empties his magazine into her. Nine loud blasts, and each shot jerks Raven.

Raven manages to get a few shots off that strike Sparrow in the vest, and he curses and stomps in circles while clutching his wound. Eventually, he falls to his knees and looks at his bloody palm.

"Ah, damn it! Damn it, damn it, damn it! One went through the vest! Fuck!" cries Sparrow. "It blocks a rifle just fine, but damn a pistol breaks this thing? Piece of shit!"

Sparrow screams again and stumbles to his feet as blood wets his pants and shirt. Robin stares at him with a small, satisfied smile that brings throbbing pain to her jaw while Sparrow approaches Raven. She is on her back, trying to grab her pistol, and blood is seeping across the filthy floor from multiple wounds on her chest, arm, and a tear on her neck.

Raven gurgles and gasps for air. Blood bubbles past her lips, and Sparrow ejects the spent magazine. He grabs Raven's gun, tosses his aside, and then he inspects her bloodied body until he retrieves the trigger for the bombs. Once he has that, he stands up and glares at Raven.

"You know, it was your mom that stabbed me in the neck with that fork in that shitty hotel room in this godforsaken tin can. Fana Black should have gone to prison for attempted murder, but OD'd in an alley instead," says

Sparrow.

Blood and tears soak Raven's pale face as she gurgles, and Sparrow aims his pistol at her head.

"Say hello to your mom for me," says Sparrow.

One more gunshot rings out, and Raven goes silent, but her feet still twitch. Seconds later, Sparrow takes a dramatic, deep breath and turns to Robin, and she stares at him, white with fear.

"Where'd that smug smile go?" asks Sparrow.

Robin stays silent, and Sparrow winces and checks his bloody palm. Then he shakes his head and rubs his bloody hand on Robin's hair.

"You're probably wondering why I'm doing this?" says Sparrow. He taps Robin's head with his pistol. "But the answer is right in that little brain of yours. You just need to think a little bit. Think back to last year."

Robin's mind races, and Sparrow's eyes bore into her like a hot drill.

"Think, Chickadee. Think. Think. Think," says Sparrow, tapping her head each time with his pistol.

Each tap makes Robin whimper, and her heart races, while her mind becomes a whirlwind of memories as she struggles to find a connection between now and last year.

"I see your brain working but work it harder!" orders Sparrow.

"I'm thinking! I promise I'm thinking!" cries Robin.

Sparrow stands up and looks down at Robin.

"Think. Harder," says Sparrow. "Think about last year. Think about what you did last year that changed lives."

"I..." Robin stops, and like a switch being flicked, she remembers clearly. The thug, the train tracks, the brutal death that she accidentally caused. Her mouth hangs open, and her eyes water as she looks up at Sparrow. "Oh my God... It can't be, yet it all makes sense now."

Sparrow smiles wickedly at Robin. "Ah, you remember, don't you?"

"I do..."

"And what did you do?"

Robin whimpers, and Sparrow kneels in front of her again and puts his pistol under her chin.

"What did you do?" repeats Sparrow.

"I accidentally killed a man. I pushed him away from me when he tried robbing me, and he fell on the tracks and got run over by a train," says Robin.

Sparrow's smile disappears. "What?"

Robin looks into Sparrow's eyes. Tears and fear meet confusion.

"You're related to the guy I accidentally killed when he tried stealing my purse!" says Robin.

Sparrow stands up, still confused. "What the hell are you talking about?"

"The guy that fell onto the tracks and got run over. You're related to him, or you knew him, right? That's why you're doing this to me, right? This is an elaborate revenge mission, right?" says Robin desperately.

Sparrow shakes his head and paces in a circle while clutching his wound.

"No... No, that's wrong. That's all wrong," says Sparrow.

"It is?" says Robin.

"It's wrong!" yells Sparrow. "I have no idea what you're talking about with a thug and a purse! If some thug died on the tracks, he deserved it for being a menace to society."

Sparrow suddenly grabs Robin's head like a striking viper and presses his pistol underneath her chin again, making her yelp and tremble.

"Think harder, Chickadee! Think of last year! Think of my face!" yells Sparrow.

"I don't know what you're talking about!" cries Robin.

"You don't remember closing the door on me!"

Robin stiffens, blinks, then her mouth falls open from shock.

"What?" says Robin.

"You closed the door on me," says Sparrow.

"When?"

"Last year!"

"I don't remember this! And even if I did, *this* kind of reaction to it is petty beyond belief!"

Sparrow stands up, glaring at Robin, and she returns the look in kind while testing the cuff.

"You're a lunatic," says Robin. "An absolute lunatic!"

"Spare me your self-righteous jargon," snaps Sparrow.

"What self-righteous jargon!? I'm not self-righteous-ing anything! You literally caused the deaths of hundreds and killed my friends because of a door! I don't even remember closing a door on anybody!"

Sparrow groans irritably and rubs his face.

"I can't believe I have to spell this out for you," says Sparrow. "You closed the door on me when I was in Lower Cepheus City. I was in the Poseidon restaurant right across from you, and I know you saw me because you looked right at me! And because you closed the door on me, I missed the elevator up, and because I missed the elevator up, I had to wait for another one. After I got to the elevator and went to the surface, I was on my way to the space port, but got cut off by a pleb which made me miss my light. Because of that, the taxi I was in got stuck at a stupid light that didn't change for ten minutes.

"Then I had trouble getting into the launch port because of bad traffic. By the time I got my parking spot and was able to get inside, I *missed* my flight! Because I missed my flight, I had to take another flight with a low-class transport that was cramped and smelly and the bathroom door wouldn't unlock, so I was stuck in a bathroom for eight hours before the attendant knew I was in there. And then when I reached *The City of Clouds*, Ibis took my room because Chick gave him **my** key.

"Because of that, I had to take a shitty hotel room with one hundred thread-count sheets, and then Raven's mom stabbed me in the neck with the fork because she was buzzed out on God knows what, and I filed a customer complaint, but they never answered, and they deleted my negative reviews on their website. And after all that shit, I found out that Jay Azure didn't even consider me for a journalism award that was being hosted **here!** And this habitat is his pride and joy. He financed its construction and expansions, and so I figured why not kill all the birds who wronged me with one stone?

"Oh, and before I forget, I hired a private investigator that found out you closed the door on me and that it was **Barfolomew** who cut me off. Then I hired a hitman to kill that private investigator, and before the hitman got his money, I shot him through the back of the head and tossed the pistol and his body in the ocean and sank the boat, so his body will never be found. Then I bribed the habitat lottery guy to bring you and Blackbird here, convinced my regional boss to let me bring Ibis along for my assignment, hired the main cook person to poison the crew, and that clerk, Chick, to have pirates sneak in before the attack for recon. Then I had the pirates kill them to cover my trail. And while the attack was happening, Raven was supposed to plant explosives in the engines of the ship and habitat, so that way the pirates would die in a freak accident after the explosives destroy the habitat engine, causing a chain reaction that would blow up the entire facility. The dead pirates were to be blamed for the tragedy, and I would to be the sole survivor, while everyone else died.

"But that didn't happen, so now you're cuffed to this railing, and you get to die with this ship! Final moments of sheer fear and terror as you watch Bellona consume you and crush you with her gravitational power as payment for your sins against me! *ANY QUESTIONS!?*"

There are a few seconds of silence, and then Robin says, "You're a dick."

Sparrow sneers. "Well, fuck you, too. I got a lifeboat to catch and some medicine to find. Try to suffer a lot for me, will you?"

Sparrow pats Robin's cheek.

"Tata," he says.

He proceeds to hobble away, leaving a trail of bloody dots in his wake, and Robin watches him go through a door on the other side of the room. When the door opens, she briefly sees a sign pointing to lifeboats down below.

Once the door closes, Robin immediately begins struggling against her cuff. Her thrashing, tugging, banging, and kicking leads to little results, and she screams in aggravation.

"Come on! Come on! Come on!" yells Robin.

This yelling and screaming brings flashes of pain to her battered face, but she doesn't quit. She will *not* be dying on this habitat. She will *not* let Sparrow get away with his terrorism.

Robin grits her teeth, presses her foot against the railing and tugs her hand against the cuff. Pain surges through her jaw as she clenches her cracked teeth.

Blood seeps past her bandages under her glove, and she stops struggling just long enough to remove said glove and to tear off her filthy bandages. She starts tugging and cursing again, and very soon her injuries break open, and her hand becomes slick with blood.

Little by little, millimeter by millimeter, Robin's hand moves through the cuff. Her skin breaks, her three-diamond markings are scratched, and her bones bend as metal and determination clash.

Blood drips to the floor, and Robin takes a moment to adjust her footing and catch a breath. Her heart is speeding like a racing horse, and she screams over the alarm as she gives one final tug. Her legs are strained, her face aches, and her hand pops free.

Robin falls flat on her back and quickly rolls to her feet, tosses aside her other glove, and tears off a piece of her torn jacket to wrap her bleeding hand. Then she grabs Blackbird's rifle, checks it, and marches after Sparrow with Bellona's light reflecting off her fiery eyes.

Sparrow will die.

And Robin will make sure of it.

Sparrow Must Die

Robin runs across the destroyed Commons Cloud, and nearly trips over herself when she enters the stairwell. Upon entering, she pushes through the disorientation caused by the noise of the alarms and flashing lights bouncing and reflecting off the walls. She bolts down the stairs, passing smeared bloody hand prints and bloody dots on the floor.

When she reaches the bottom, she doesn't wait for the door to open all the way before going through. But she immediately seeks cover behind a pillar when she hears gunshots.

Then she hears more gunshots and peeks out to see Sparrow shooting at the windows of the lifeboats with his pistol. One round for each window. While Sparrow is distracted shooting another window, Robin slides out of cover and shoots Sparrow.

He yelps and falls back, knocking over a tool cart. The tools scatter, and Robin's breathing is unsteady as she rapidly approaches him.

Sparrow scrambles for cover behind a lifeboat when Robin tries shooting him again, and when she rounds the ship, Sparrow screams and swings a hammer at her. She blocks with the rifle, but the strike knocks her weapon out of her hands, and Sparrow swings at her head.

Robin ducks and pushes him against the lifeboat. They roll off its hull, leaving thick streaks of blood, and Sparrow kicks Robin away and breathes heavily as he grabs a wrench.

Robin attempts to grab her rifle, but Sparrow kicks it away, and then kicks her on her back. He goes for a strike with his wrench, but she rolls out of the way, causing him to lose his balance.

Sparrow stumbles to recover, and Robin grabs a screwdriver and screams as she stabs him in the side. Sparrow also screams, and he trips over himself and drags Robin with him to the floor. They roll around, and Sparrow yanks out the screwdriver and stabs Robin.

Robin gasps and gags, and Sparrow headbutts her, rolls her to the bottom, grabs her head, and slams it on the floor. Robin's ears ring and her vision spins, and Sparrow staggers away from her, pale and shaking, and his body wet with blood.

"Man, Crow was right. You are a roach," says Sparrow.

Sparrow then hobbles away, using a lifeboat for support, and Robin holds her wound while shifting to sit on her knees, and she watches with narrowed eyes through her bloodied and sweaty locks as Sparrow seals himself inside the only lifeboat not shot. He flips Robin the bird, and then goes to the driver's seat.

"No…" groans Robin.

Sparrow buckles in, and Robin pushes herself up.

"No," repeats Robin.

Sparrow turns on his lifeboat. Its engines hum and the exhaust ports glow blue. Robin falls over when she grabs her rifle. An energy barrier activates as the airlock slides open, revealing the Section 0 ship nearby and Bellona behind it. The red light pours into the airlock, and streaks of lightning surge across the gas giant's bands and reflect off Robin's eyes as she aims her rifle at the lifeboat.

The lifeboat surges forward and Robin screams, "No!"

She pulls the trigger, and sparks fly off the lifeboat as the bullets strike it. Bursts of fire pop from the back before the lifeboat exits, but the it keeps going. Robin drops to her knees, clutching her wound and crying as she watches Sparrow's lifeboat fly to the Section 0 ship.

"No…" whimpers Robin.

*****

Inside the lifeboat, Sparrow cackles weakly and pulls out Raven's detonator while warning alarms sound off and displays of engine failure and compromised life support plaster the screen. But he doesn't care. The Section 0 ship is nearby. They'll pick him up soon, *and* he accomplished his mission. Everyone responsible for the worst day of his life has paid in blood for their crimes against him.

He pushes the detonator and–

*****

The multitude of bombs placed around the Engine Cloud are detonated in a synchronized manner. Fire and shrapnel rips apart the pipes, fans, and safety barriers. The hourglass-shaped machines in the center flicker and power surges throughout *The City of Clouds*.

*****

The City of Clouds shakes violently, and Robin is thrown to the ground as sparks fall from the flickering lights and the energy barrier separating her and space weakens. During the shake up, Robin notices a maintenance tube with an engineer suit. She grits her teeth, pulls out the screwdriver in her, and hobbles towards it as fast as she can, occasionally losing balance as the habitat shakes.

*****

In the Commons Cloud, a surge of power and fire blows apart the pipes and shatters the damaged dome. Corpses, debris, and Bellona's statue are sucked into space, and–

*****

Sparrow tosses the detonator aside, rubs his bloody hands and tries to move the lifeboat, but the steering doesn't work. He frowns and jiggles the steering stick and smashes buttons, not noticing the warning signs flashing on the screen. But what he does notice is Bellona's statue spinning towards him.

"You've got to be kidding me," says Sparrow.

And that was his final words before the spearhead of the statue pierces the lifeboat and puts it in a spin that takes Sparrow directly to Bellona's gravity well; where he is consumed by the gas giant's storm.

*****

Robin uses the screwdriver and a hammer to break the safety latches on the tube, and she grunts and trembles as she pries it open. Then she mutters and whimpers as she rushes to put on the suit.

Her slick hands drop pieces of it, and she falls over when she tries slipping into the suit. She screams as an electric surge blows out the lights, plunging her darkness, save for the faint glow of the barrier and Bellona's light. But even she can see the barrier is failing.

Robin zips up her suit, and coughs blood when she grabs her gloves.

A distant explosion rattles the ship, and Robin looks outside as she tightens the glove straps. She sees the Section 0 ship adjusting its position as a large chunk of *The City of Clouds* spirals by, leaving a trail of wreckage.

Another explosion shakes the habitat, and Robin slips on her helmet. The helmet seals around her neck with a series of clicks and hisses, and Robin grabs a jetpack on the rack. Right as she grabs it, a large explosion tears through the hangar, breaking the barrier generators. There is a jarring tug that pulls Robin into space and suffocates the fire.

Robin shrieks and clutches her jetpack tight while lifeboats, tools, and broken metal spin past her. Pieces of *The City of Clouds* break apart and lights flicker and flash as rolling fire surges through its pathways, decimating it from the inside out. Sections of the habitat pop or snap loose and their pieces spin off into the void, and Robin holds her jetpack tighter as she uses it to evade the debris.

She bounces off a particularly large piece of metal, and almost loses her grip on her device, but she quickly regains a good grip and launches herself over a gutted pathway. And she keeps going up until she is a grain of white in a black sea, and she watches the chaos with her good eye wide and tears cleaning the blood and grime off her face.

Fire and bursts of energy keep tearing apart *The City of Clouds*, and she sees a small, sleek aircraft speeding towards her. It's a striker craft.

Robin's face hurts when she smiles, and she uses her jetpack to push herself closer to it. The striker craft swoops by her, and its back opens as a ramp, where a soldier in an all-black spacesuit tied to a tether jumps out to her, using a jetpack on his suit.

He extends his hand to her, and she reaches out and grabs it. The tether is recoiled at great speed, and both are brought inside.

Robin stumbles when her feet touch the metal, and the ramp lifts and seals them inside the ship.

"Survivor is rescued! Hit the gas!" orders the soldier that brought her in.

The strike craft rumbles, and the soldier holds Robin and a handrail. There are a couple more soldiers in full body suits who also grab their handrail, and Robin's legs buckle as the strike craft surges forward. The ship rattles and its light flickers, while Robin's skin and hair feels like it is being overwhelmed with static electricity as a bright blue light bleeds through the windows of the cockpit.

But as quickly as the light came, it fades. The sharp tingles disappear, the strike craft slows down, and Robin's legs give out as she coughs blood in her helmet. The soldier eases her into a chair and quickly removes her helmet. When he sees her bloodied condition he points at the nearest person.

"Get the medical kit!" orders the soldier. He looks at Robin and grips her shoulder tightly. "It's going to be okay, ma'am. We're going to take care of you."

"Yes... please do... I'm on vacation," says Robin.

Then she slumps over and blacks out.

The End

Robin's eye cracks open to the sound of faint chatter and footsteps. She is briefly blinded by the light, but the scenery gradually form. First, it is the lamp above her. Then, it is the metallic ceiling and its vent.

She tilts her head and sees a tower of monitors displaying vitals and visuals of her heart and lungs. Beyond that is a white wall with pictures of human anatomy.

Robin turns her head to the other wall and sees posters depicting proper procedures and emergency numbers.

Robin looks back at the ceiling and realizes that she can't feel anything. There's no pain, no weight, no soreness, nothing. She tries lifting her hand, but finds her arm is strapped down, and in her arm are IVs attached to a device gently pumping fluids into her body. She tries her other arm, and that one lifts just fine.

Upon lifting her arm, she sees her hand is professionally bandaged, but she can't move her fingers. She winces and stiffly brings her hand to her face. But since her fingers are stuck in an open position by small casts, her fingers feel a rake rubbing against her face.

While feeling her face, Robin realizes that half of it is bandaged, and the portion that isn't bandaged has gauze and medical tape covering parts of her exposed skin.

Then a doctor carrying a pad calmly walks in. Robin watches him go to the tower of monitors, and he checks to make sure the information matches what is on his pad. Once that is done, he looks at Robin with a practiced smile.

"You're lucky. If we hadn't detected you floating out in space, you would have died in that suit," says the doctor.

Robin is quiet, and the doctor makes an exaggerated, sympathetic sigh and puts his hand on her shoulder.

"But the good news is that the worst of it is over. You're safe now. We'll have you treated before we drop you off at Andromeda, and then they can handle your rehab."

"What about the other passengers?" croaks Robin.

The doctor bobs his head. "Eh, they're fine. Some got a little bruised, but they're mostly just shaken up. They'll probably have PTSD, which is something drugs and distractions can easily fix. They'll get over it in no time. But you are top priority in care since you were on the brink of death. You'll need some rehab on Andromeda since the adrenaline coursing through your body blocked out your brain registering all the damaged bones and internal bleeding you had. Fortunately, the surgery fixed those problems."

Robin looks at the doctor, at a loss for words, and the doctor forces a smile and pats her shoulder.

"Rest easy, and don't worry about the bill. This one is on the house as a thank you for being an upstanding citizen of the Federation of Sol Systems," says the doctor.

He briskly exits the room after that, and once he is out of sight, Robin rests her head on the pillow and looks at the ceiling again. She wants to cry for Ibis and Blackbird, but she can't do it. She is too numb. She can't even bring herself to worry if Sparrow made it or not. All she has is a foggy mind and a body too fatigued to move. Straps not helping.

Really, Robin is hoping all of this is just a terrible nightmare and that she is still on *The City of Clouds*, bored out of her skull, and just taking a nap. She doesn't even want to imagine what would happen next if everything that had happened was in fact real.

A sudden knock on the door frame takes Robin out of her thoughts, and she strains her neck to see who it is. She's not sure who she's looking at, but he is in the military, wearing a dark operational uniform with a "o" patch on his shoulders that is a Blackbeard skull with a sword through it. His silver name tag saying "Stripe."

"May I come in?" he asks.

Robin nods, and the man enters. Robin watches him approach, and wonders if she's the butt of a joke. He's athletic, blonde hair and blue-eyed, like her preferred type on the dating apps. The mystery man grabs a nearby stool and gently sets it down next to her.

"Are you doing okay?" he asks.

Robin barely shakes her head. Now tears are burning her eyes, and her throat becomes stuffed with a wet blob. She doesn't want to admit it, but she knows what she is seeing is real. What she experienced is real. Her friends are dead, she needs rehab, and now she won't be able to function in society.

And seeing how what happened was an insane event, she'll probably be hounded for the rest of her days by people who want to hear her story so they can profit off her pain.

"Ma'am?" asks the soldier.

"No... I'm not," says Robin hoarsely.

Stripe nods slowly in understanding, and he wrings his hands.

"I understand," he says. "I just wanted to say that I'm the one that pulled you in the strike craft, and I've been worried about you since you've been in and out for days. Not only are you a civilian, but you're a clone, so you're not exactly built tough."

Robin stares at him, and he awkwardly adjusts his position.

"Well, I mean, you're a tough clone. Probably a glitch in the genetic coding that popped up when you were in the vat since your clone model is prone to heart failure. But what you survived was amazing. You should be happy. Proud even," says Stripe.

"I'm not," says Robin weakly.

Stripe scrunches his brow. "Why not?"

"Because my friends are dead."

Stripe blinks. "Oh... I'm sorry to hear that."

"I shouldn't be alive. I'm a mass-produced product. Good only for vanity and advertisement. Bartholomew Blackbird should have lived. Ibis Ajam should have lived. They're special in that they were human. I was grown in a lab. They came from nature."

"Hey," says Stripe. He puts his hand on Robin's shoulder and looks her in the eyes. "Don't go thinking like that. You lived because you fought to live, and if they were anything like you, they also fought hard. Your survival is amazing, and as long as you keep going forward and living, you can live for them. And I know what you're going through. I've lost friends on the field, too."

"Even to random pirate attacks and betrayal?" asks Robin.

"Well, my unit is the one that attacks the pirates, and there have been deaths on duty, as well as betrayal. It's unfortunate, but it happens, and it is never easy to get over," says Stripe.

He pulls out a notebook from his pocket and scribbles down some information, and after looking around, he slips it under Robin's pillow while offering a quick apology.

"I know this is awkward, but my name is Jack Stripe. My number and email are on that paper. If you want to talk or need advice on anything, I'll be there," says Stripe.

Robin is silent, and Stripe sighs heavily and stands up. After adjusting his uniform, he returns the stool to its original spot and nods to Robin.

"Sleep well, ma'am," says Stripe.

Robin swallows and blinks tears out of her eyes, and Stripe takes another breath, before walking towards the door.

"Wait," says Robin.

Stripe stops and looks at her. Robin swallows again and takes a few seconds to muster up her words. Even after she gathers her words, she still hesitates.

"Will you please come back?" asks Robin.

Stripe smiles thinly. "Will do."

Then he exits the room, and Robin lets herself go limp in the bed. She takes a deep, long breath, and then she closes her eyes and goes to sleep.

-THE END-

About the Author

One day I was born and decided to just roll with it.

You can connect with me on:
- 🌐 https://jbwritesstuff.blog
- 🐦 https://twitter.com/CarolinaTreeEqn
- 🔗 https://www.minds.com/palmettohorse

Also by J.B. Williams

Action packed sci-fi adventures! From parasitic plant monsters destroying a colony ship, to government agents having their memories manipulated in a post war world!

Bon Voyage (Second Edition)
Ethan Rifts tries to start over as an untrained medic on an AATS ship, but when a distress signal from a colony ship is intercepted, his team is plunged into a nightmare involving an unknown alien species and psychotic survivors.

Aarde
Agent 505, Holden Hosenheim, becomes the targets of rebels and the government agency he worked for when he finds out his memories have been altered.